D1526306

Indigo After Dark

Genesis Press's new imprint goes beyond sensuous. It's romantic erotica that is tasteful, classy and vividly sexual—in short, it's hot but not pornographic. Here's what some of the readers had to say about *Indigo After Dark.*

"The stories give just the right amount of tease to entice the reader to breathe hard and wish to be inside the pages of the book."

"I'm in my twelfth year of marriage, and reading these stories gives me plenty of ideas and helps me to re-create the romance that has dwindled away."

"MORE, MORE, MORE! This is exactly what I've been waiting for—African-American romance. Bravo, Genesis!"

"This is great!! It's erotic without being vulgar. I can't wait until this line is on the bookshelves."

"Romantic, yes, but even more so, in a sexy, romantic type of fantasy. These stories seem to be geared toward a more mature female reader, like myself."

"I think this is just what we need, some seduction along with some romance. I'll definitely buy this book."

"The sexual overtures were a turn-on. It's nice to know that passion exists between two people."

So go on, what are you waiting for? Your fantasies await you on the other side of this page. Indulge.

Indigo After Dark

is published by

Genesis Press, Inc.
315 Third Avenue North
Columbus, MS 39701

Indigo After Dark, Vol. III
Pant & Impulse

First Edition

Caution:

Reading this book causes extreme stimulation, lust and exquisite languor.

Brought to you by

Indigo After Dark

an Imprint of

Genesis Press, Inc.

Indigo After Dark

Vol. III

Romantic Erotica... for Women

Genesis Press, Inc.

Indigo After Dark...
Beyond Sensuous

Vol. III

Pant
by
Coco Morena

Impulse
by
Montana Blue

Table of Contents

Pant by Coco Morena
PART I

Impulse by Montana Blue
PART II

Pant

by
Coco Morena

The More Things Change...

On the first night after Carl and I broke up, I was happy. You know what I felt? I felt free. I felt like I could finally do all the things I had been longing to do secretly in the back of mind. I felt like I could finally take a trip to Vegas with my girls and flirt and laugh and not worry about checking in. I could finally go have a beer without writing a full dissertation first. I felt like I could wear low-cut shirts and a push-up bra to my job and give my old, decrepit boss a reason to live. I could shove twenties down the G-strings of male strippers and not have to account for why I couldn't pay the light bill. I could go to a ballet, or a puppet show for that matter, and not be worried about whether or not Carl was liking it. I felt like I was free to dance. To move. To travel. To lust. To remodel.

That night, as I lay between the cool sheets alone, I was happy to have the bed to myself. I was happy to be fantasizing about my life as a single Vegas showgirl. And I knew, somewhere in the back of my mind that I would see Carl again tomorrow. And tomorrow night he would be lying next to me again, making the bed all hot, and things would be back the way they were supposed to be. Carl and I, after all, were supposed to be. There are just some things you don't mess with; some things that never change.

But on the second night I was still in my bed alone. And my fantasies about all the things I would do without him crumbled, dissolved into stupid, inane dreams that meant nothing. I cried until my head banged. I paged him fifty times. I ate half a gallon of chocolate chip cookie dough ice cream. And, at about dawn, I crawled out of the bed and lay on the floor, wrapped up in a sheet next to Azure, the dog.

Two months later, there I was again. Because that is how I had spent every night for the past nine weeks. I always started off in the bed. But it was so cold, and so lonely. And Carl had taken everything that was his. He took every shirt, every photo, every poster, every book, every sock. So as far as anyone new could tell, there had never been a Carl living in my house. Sleeping in my bed. There was just Azure and me. And I think Carl would have taken him, too, if his new woman had allowed pets in her apartment.

I amazed myself that I was able every morning to pull myself up off the floor and put on a suit and go to work. I was amazed that I didn't die right there on the carpet. Or pass out in the shower. Or crash on the highway daydreaming and missing my man.

"Oh, Steph. You look like hell," Tracy said one morning as I dragged my briefcase and gym bag into the office behind me. She was receptionist; the ever vigilant keeper of the gate to Zimiles, Inc. She never missed a beat. She knew everything about everybody and, except for telling me everybody's business because we were friends, she kept secrets pretty well.

"Thanks. You know, I try." I smirked and slumped down in a chair in the office lobby.

"You know you have a meeting with Herbie Morales at ten?" If she hadn't told me what I was supposed to be doing and when for the past two months, I would have surely been fired. I was barely making it there. Everything else was extra.

"Herbie? Oh, the guy from La Plaza Beer? Crap!" I remembered now that I was supposed to be pitching him his new ad campaign today. I also remembered that I hadn't thought twice about that damn nasty beer since we had signed him two weeks ago.

"So what's your slogan?" Tracy asked me. Was she kidding? My slogan at the moment was "I want my man back." I wasn't thinking about any beer, unless I was drowning my sorrows in it.

" I don't have one," I admitted.

"Oh. You are so fired. Zimiles is gonna have your head."

"Well, maybe I can come up with something in an hour. The beer tastes like piss. What am I supposed to say?"

"I don't know but you look like hell. Walk me to the bathroom and let's try not to scare away the rest of the clients." She walked out the double doors to the hallway, and I followed.

"La Plaza beer," I said in the bathroom, "tastes the same coming out as it does going in."

"Forget it. You want High Kickin' Wine or Golden Lady?" she asked, handing me two tubes of lipstick.

"Wine," I answered. "Okay. How about: The only beer that's one hundred percent recyclable."

"Is your résumé done? I could type it up for you."

"Okay, then. How about: La Plaza Beer, If you drink enough, the taste won't matter."

"You might wanna do a little something to your hair. You're getting fired. You don't need to look fired, too."

Finally I gave up. "You're right. It's over. I quit." I let out a sigh and slumped into the chair in the bathroom lounge. We were never supposed to sit in this chair since Tracy had heard that our 150-year-old, possibly bisexual boss had given oral sex to the twenty-two-year-old office manager on this very spot. But this was a special occasion. I was officially broken.

"You know what?" Tracy said, smiling. "That High Kickin' Wine looks fab on you. Let's take a trip."

"A trip to where?" I asked. I didn't want to take any damn trip. A trip to my bed was all. I wanted to take a trip to the couch and watch the guests on today's controversial talk shows and anybody else who was as miserable as I was.

"I don't know. Miami. Bahamas. Jamaica. Somewhere. You need to get up out of this rut. You have to find yourself again, Stephanie. Carl is gone."

"And you feel the need to keep reminding me? I don't wanna go anywhere. I'm not Stella."

"No. But you definitely need your groove back. And some nice blue water and a fine Jamaican bartender looking for citizenship might do just that."

"Forget it," I told her and got up to go face my music.

"I'm booking the trip today." She was an implacable little something. But that was another reason that I liked her.

It happened, by the grace of God, that Herbie Morales and his pee-flavored cerveza canceled our appointment. Apparently a bad batch of La Plaza had to be recalled, and he was up to his ears in lawsuit threats and health inspectors. I went home early and fell out on my couch. It was only by reflex that I answered the phone because I sure didn't want to talk.

"We leave on Monday," Tracy's voice said. I already paid for it on my charge and put in for vacation, so you have to go. You have to pay me back, too. But you have to go."

And, on Monday morning, Tracy and I were landing in Montego Bay, Jamaica. Shit. I didn't want to be in anybody's Jamaica.

The Moonlight Beach Hotel and Resort was much prettier in the books. And the men on the commercials were much finer. And the ladies in the Come Back to Jamaica ads were much nicer. The three women behind the counter all rolled their eyes at us when we went to check in. "Your room is not ready, yet," one said.

"Why not?" Tracy asked.

"Because it's not," the woman retorted.

"Oh no! Let me tell you something..." I started but Tracy pulled me away.

"Let's just wait at the bar."

There were five bars altogether at the hotel. And between the rum, the free jerk chicken and the water, I was a lot calmer when we finally got our room.

It was only so-so really. Hard tile floors, old fixtures in the bathroom, one queen-size bed instead of the two we requested. It was almost more depressing than being at home. Even the cable wasn't working.

"I'm going on the nude beach," Tracy said, coming out of the bathroom in her bathing suit. There were three beaches in all: a family beach, a topless beach and a nude section that was separated from the others by a beach bar and some rocks.

"You're lying," I flagged her

"See ya." She waved and walked out the door.

I lay there on the bed for a moment. I had always wanted to come to Jamaica. But I had always wanted to be here with Carl, not crazy Tracy. I missed him. I missed his touch. His heat. His smile. I couldn't even remember what it was exactly that had broken us up. I got up off the bed and put on my own yellow bikini. Perhaps I would venture as far as topless, but that was it.

I took a magazine and headed down to the beach. I thought about a beer but the local Red Stripe was worse than Herbie's La Plaza, so I laid out with a glass of pineapple juice and watched middle-aged white women with sagging breasts slather themselves in tanning oil and beg for attention.

I thought about going topless, I even went so far as to unhook the bra, but I didn't let it fall.

"If you take that top off, I would die today a happy man."

5

Say what? I knew that voice. I turned around to face a beautiful set of dark brown pectoral muscles. *Mercy!* I thought before my eyes even made it up to the face.

"Christopher!" I screamed and jumped up, and the top of my bathing suit fell to the sand. I couldn't decide whether to hug him or hide myself so I tried to do both. He laughed and handed me my top. "What are you doing here?" I asked, hooking my top back together.

Christopher Edwards was my boyfriend from the seventh grade all the way through high school. And since I was a little fast, he also managed to rob me of my virginity when I was about fourteen. He was beautiful; he had always been. But now, with age and hard work came a body that I couldn't believe. Muscles came at me from everywhere. Even when I tried to look at something that would not remind me of how fine he was, that part was fine, too. I couldn't look at his chest so I looked in his eyes. I couldn't look in his eyes so I watched his lips. I couldn't watch his lips so I stared at his abs and his legs and his feet. Even his feet, I tell you! Even his feet!

"I missed you, you know," he said to me. "I always told you to call me if you needed me. You never called."

"Well, Carl wouldn't have liked that," I answered honestly. I had missed him, too. Maybe. But I was no cheat.

"Well, where is good ol' Carl now? Back in the room with you out here almost naked?" They had never liked each other. Ever. Chris was jealous that Carl had won me. And Carl was jealous of the time Christopher and I had without him.

"I don't know where Carl is. He's gone."

"Too bad," he answered. "Cause I'm here now."

Christopher was in Jamaica on business. His company was in the process of buying beachfront property for a sports resort just down the street from the Moonlight Beach. We walked and talked all afternoon. We were catching up and reminiscing about braces and basement parties and cheerleading and senior proms. We talked about college and jobs and ex-wives and one-night stands. We didn't keep secrets. It felt so good. And, oh, he looked so good. His voice was deep and soothing. It seemed to soothe away all of my pain. Before it seemed like an hour, it was after seven, and we found ourselves in a coral cove with a small deserted beach and the moon came up right in front of us.

"How come you didn't marry me?" he asked. "I always thought it would've been me."

"You never asked, Chris," I said.

"I won't make that mistake again," he told me, and he leaned over and kissed me on the mouth. My eyes rolled to the back of my head, and my heart stopped beating. His lips were so full and soft and hot. I opened my mouth a little just to feel his warmth a little more, and he shoved his huge tongue inside and licked my teeth. Something between my stomach and my crotch woke up and did a dance. I could feel myself beginning to steam between my legs, and I pulled away.

"What's wrong?" he asked.

"Nothing. It's just..."

"It's okay," he said, tracing my eyebrow lightly with his finger. "You don't have to do anything. I know it's been a long time. Let me do everything." He kissed me again on the lips and then on my chin and then again on my neck. Everywhere he kissed seemed to burn even after he had moved his mouth away. He was sitting on the edge of my beach chair, and he slid down and kissed my chest and then licked around the edge of my bathing suit top. My nipples got up and ran around the chair screaming hallelujah. I thought he was going to lift my top but he didn't. He just kept kissing everything that wasn't covered. I moaned and I smiled but I didn't do anything. Just like he said. He scooted down a little more and licked my stomach down to the edge of my yellow bikini bottoms.

"You look so good laying here on this beach," he whispered to me. "I've been wanting to do this all day." He bit my hip softly, and my body shook without my permission. "I've been wanting to make love to you for so long," he said. And then he touched me. And, oh my god! His huge, strong hands moved from my hair to my face and over my breasts. They massaged and they squeezed and they pulled and they brought my whole body back to life. Then they rested on my hips, and he moved his face between my legs and took a deep breath in through his nose.

"Oh, baby. You smell so good. I just want to taste you," he whispered. "I just want to remember how good you taste."

He took his fingers and pulled the strings on my bikini bottoms down over my hips. My back arched naturally to make it easier, but my brain was going bananas. Oh, this isn't happening. This isn't real. This isn't happening. Oh...my...god... How can he...what about...but when we...

Then he pushed my knees apart and rubbed his nose up against my clit. A river began to form somewhere in the mountains inside my body. He opened his hot, wet mouth and placed it over the entrance to my womb. I shook again. He stayed there for a moment just letting the heat from inside of him flow inside of me. Then, just as I was getting used to his face being between my legs, he aimed his huge, massively solid tongue straight forward and up into my body. I didn't know whether to laugh or cry so I just screamed. He gripped my hips in his hands and pulled them toward his face. He licked inside of my walls until I thought he had hit the top. Then he pulled his tongue out and began to swirl it in soft circles around my clit, still gripping my hips is his hands. *Damn!* I thought. I couldn't think any whole comprehensible phrases. Damn wasn't saying anything and yet it was enough. He licked around the outside of my pussy until I had cum a hundred times. Then he went back in for the kill. He rammed his tongue inside me as though it were his penis, which in itself I remembered to be beautiful and shiny and tremendously solid. I wanted him so bad. I wanted to feel his dick up in me. I wanted him to take me back to seventeen. To the days I used to crawl up the walls because he was too big. To the days I was bent over the railing on the back porch giving it up from behind. I wanted him inside me but he just kept going in and out and in and out with his tongue, pulling my hips toward his face. I didn't want to move but I couldn't help it. And he wanted me to. So I arched my back and moved my hips up to meet his mouth. Back and forth and then in small, concentrated circles until I felt the quivering down inside my lips move up to my stomach and into my brain. I grabbed his thick, curly hair with two hands and pulled his face even deeper into me. I could feel his chin rubbing the soft spot between my ass and the well that was pouring out juices by the gallon. I could feel his nose tickling my clit and his lips and teeth and tongue all over my pussy. He went from being locked between my legs to being everywhere. He was down there. He was up here. He was behind me and in front of me. He was in the sand. He was in the sky. My hips rocked faster and faster, and he licked and ate and sucked and pulled just as fast as I needed him to, until I was empty and breathless and he was full.

We stayed on the beach the whole night, watching the sun replace the moon, and, eventually, falling asleep both in the same chair.

"Christopher is here," I told Tracy when I finally got back to the room. "I spent the whole night with him on the beach. He wants me to go out with him today."

"Did you get some?" she asked, and I looked at her sideways.

"Not exactly but I got something." I smiled. " I got something." And I went into the bathroom and got into the shower.

That day Christopher and I went to the spa on the resort and got massages and manicures. Christopher had awakened something within me because I couldn't even sit still through my massage without having an orgasm.

"Are you okay?" the woman kept asking. And I kept telling her I was fine but eventually I had to make her stop.

Christopher just laughed at me. "You let that massage lady turn you on?"

"No," I told him. "You turned me on. Now I just can't turn myself off."

We took a cab almost two hours to Rick's café in Negril and drank strawberry daiquiris until we could have floated back to the resort. I smoked a Cuban cigar. Chris danced a freaky native dance with the pleasantly plump lady who was the lead singer in the reggae cover band. When they played "Turn the Lights Down Low," he came up behind me and wrapped his arms around my waist. We watched the stars shimmering over the water and swayed back and forth, him grinding up against me, me drowning in his arms.

"Stay in my room tonight," he said. It wasn't a question. It was the way it was going to be. Confident and assured. I liked that in a man.

His room was a lot better than ours. He had a rug and a clock and a stereo and a new bathroom. He even had working cable with all the premium channels.

Oh, we got jipped, I thought, spreading my legs out on his king-size bed. *This is great.*

"Lie down," he told me, and I did. He turned off the lights and opened the curtain to the balcony. All the stars ever made shined into the room. I closed my eyes, and he turned me gently over onto my stomach. I heard him moving around and then I could feel something warm dripping onto my back. It was sweet like brown sugar and almonds and I liquefied into the spread. He moved his hands across my back slowly, kneading and rubbing and massaging all my cares away. The scent of the oil filled the room and dulled my brain. Other parts of my body tingled and pleaded to be rubbed next. For the past twenty-four hours, I hadn't had a careful thought. Job? What job? Carl? Carl who?

"Stephanie," Christopher spoke softly now but he was not whispering. "I really missed you."

"I really missed you, too," I said. But I didn't know if that was altogether true. I had been married. I had loved my husband. But now that I was here, I guessed that I did miss Christopher all those years... at least some.

"Good," he said, flipping me over onto my back. He poured the oil onto my stomach and then slid his hands up to my breasts. He squeezed them, and they thanked him by standing at attention. "Do you still love me?" he asked. It was a like a car came screeching through the room. Huh?

"Well, I..." I didn't get a chance to answer. He put his finger to my lips.

"Never mind. It doesn't matter. You're here...with me. If you don't love me now, you will again." I didn't want to answer him. I didn't want to tell him that I had spent many a night dreaming about touching him one more time. That over the years I had fantasized about running into him in the mall or at the market or at the company party conveniently held at the airport Ramada. But it was Carl that I loved. It was Carl who I vowed to be devoted to and to take care of and to build worlds with. It was Carl I was supposed to be with. Another car came screeching through the room with a big neon sign on it that said "But Carl's not here!" *You're right*, I thought. *Carl's not here. And Chris is. And feeling damn good right about now.*

I didn't want to talk anymore. And, in Chris' eyes, I could see that talking was not first on his agenda either. So I kissed him. I kissed him softly, mouth closed, on the lips. And then I slid my tongue between them and licked his teeth. He squeezed my hand, and I stood and gently laid him down on the bed. He closed his eyes and let out a deep breath. He had been waiting for me for a long time. And tonight he was going to have me. All of me.

I unbuttoned his linen shirt and tried to hide my smile. He was so beautifully constructed: every muscle sitting neatly and powerfully on top of the next. His nipples looked at me and so I touched them and felt them rise under my fingers. He moaned a little. I put my mouth over one and began to suck on it softly, licking around it and then flicking it with my tongue. I could see his manhood struggling to stay inside his pants.

I undid his belt and his zipper and his shaft, still huge and beautiful and shiny, just like I remembered, jumped up out of his shorts. I slid him out of his jeans and Jockeys and began to pour the same sweet almond oil on his stomach. I rubbed it on his chest and around his abs. He bent his legs up on the bed, and I sat between them rubbing his thighs and calves and feet. Then I took his instrument into my hands and stroked it between my palms, letting the oil warm up around it, every once in a while including his heavy testicles in the motion. Without letting go, I went back to kissing him.

I kissed his hot, sweet-tasting mouth. I swirled my tongue around his and sucked on his thick, masculine lips. I kissed his strong, Drakkar-scented shoulders and neck. I sucked on his nipples again and moved my tongue down the space that separated his right ab muscles from his left until I got to the bottom.

His dick was so beautiful I wanted to save it for last but I could not. I touched it gently to my face and smelled him. He was so manly and sexy and strong. He was beautiful from the shine on his hair to the scent on his dick. I put it to my mouth and slapped it lightly against my tongue. He let out a hard breath. I licked around the top of his giant mushroom in circles at first. Then I flattened my tongue and licked the whole shaft from base to tip as if it were a huge chocolate ice cream cone. It had been so long since Chris and I made love. His smile was the same but the rest was not familiar, and I was learning his ins and outs all over again.

Finally I tried to put his whole instrument in my mouth. Just the thought of being able to climb on top of him later was creating an ocean between my legs. He was so big that I couldn't take all of him in at once. I had to coax him in slowly, stretching my mouth up over the fat part and then swirling my tongue around it carefully.

As my throat relaxed, I let him farther and farther in. I held his dick in my hands, both hands, and moved them together up and down on it, gently meeting my mouth and then pulling away. He cursed and screamed from the top of the bed. I jerked his shaft faster and faster, and my mouth slid over it, easily now, pre-orgasm juices foaming in my hands. Then I pulled away before it was too late. He opened his eyes just in time to see me climbing on top of him. I put his dick up against the dripping entrance to my pussy. I could feel my own heat rising, and I knew he could feel it, too.

"Oh. Let me in, Steph. Let me feel you. Let me inside you," he begged. I smiled. And sat down on him slowly, just enough for his huge head to slip inside. I held on to his manhood from the base and rode the head of his dick all by itself. I went in and almost out a hundred times before he finally banged his heavy arms down on my shoulders forcing himself to slam farther into me. I screamed. It hurt so bad and at the same time I came all over his balls, drenching them with a bottle of lust that hadn't been opened in months.

His penis was huge, and it filled me from tip to tip. I moved up and down on it slowly at first but it was so big I couldn't move any faster without breaking something important. Internal damage was of no concern to Chris. He flipped us over and, with one arm down on the bed and one arm pulling my hair, he leaned into me over and over. When my sensibilities returned, I began to move my hips to meet him. I grabbed his tight round ass and held on for dear life. He withdrew and stroked his penis up against the outside of my pussy, and I begged him to stick it back inside me. "Please," I heard myself saying. "Please give it to me. Please let me feel it." I opened my eyes. He was smiling. And then he gave it to me. He pressed himself into me so hard that I lost my breath.

"Is this what you wanted?" he demanded. " Is this what you've been missing? Is this the dick you've been waiting for all these years?"

"Yes! " I said, halfway between agony and ecstasy. It was too much. It was just too much dick. And yet I wanted it all. All of it, all up inside me as far as it would go. "Yes," I said again. "Give it all to me. Give me that dick I've been missing, baby." He pulled out and flipped me over onto my stomach and slid his instrument right back in. I dipped my back and stuck my ass out so he could climb on. He pulled my hair and rammed me into the headboard. With my body smashed against the wood, he had me right where he wanted me. I couldn't scoot back. I couldn't move up. He pinned me right up against the board and ripped into me from behind. He pulled on my hair and whispered things I couldn't understand into my ear. I yelled at the top of my lungs, not caring that the screen was open or if the other tourists could hear me. The idea that they may be watching or listening just heightened my arousal, and I began to cum on him over and over. Hot white icing slid down our legs. My pussy contracted and pulsed on him and, when he felt my walls caving, he rammed himself into me one more hard time and pulled out, dripping cream-colored I missed you's all over my back.

Christopher and I screwed for four days and three nights. He was loving me. And a man loving me was something I had really missed.

"Girl, I don't know what I'm gonna do. I'm supposed to see him on Saturday but Zimiles is already pissed because we took vacation early, and I have a lot of work to do," I said to Tracy over the phone a few days after we got back. Azure heard something on the front porch and began to bark. He was in attack mode when Carl let himself back into the house. "It's just me, Azure," he assured the dog. "It's just Daddy, boy."

I hung up the phone with Tracy and walked into the living room where my estranged husband and my dog both stood looking at me pitifully.

"I wanna come home, Steph," Carl said. "I really missed you. I love you so much. I don't even know why we were fighting now, but I really love you. Please let's work it out. You're my wife. It's us, Steph. It's always been us. Please," he said. He took a step forward. I took a step back.

Azure barked.

"You're not in this, " I told the dog. But his eyes moved quickly back and forth between me and Carl, and he whined at me as if to say, "Can I keep him?"

"Carl, I..." I wanted to say: I have someone else. Go away. You should never have left me. You should have been back months ago. I'm in love with another man. But the truth was I was in love with my husband. I had always been. Carl and I were real, and we were supposed to be together. I loved him, and I wanted him to stay. I wrapped my arms around my husband, and I kissed his face and his neck and his ears and his hair and I thanked God that he had come home. We made love, and we made love again. And we didn't talk about our time apart. I didn't ask about the woman he had been staying with. And he didn't ask about the "We Be Jammin' in Jamaica" shirt I was wearing. And I didn't see Christopher again. Carl and I started our life over. Because when something is supposed to be, it just is. Like I said, there are some things you just don't mess with. Some things that you just can't change.

Lady of the House

I came in the house and plopped myself down on the couch. Life was getting a little too hard. I was in my second year out of college and gigging as a barmaid at Fat Harry's until my big break as an actress finally broke. But Harry was cutting hours and splitting tips, and my past three checks had been short. The only reason I stayed was because he didn't care about auditions and coming late and leaving early. The job sucked. I hated it. And I was broke.

Then, to add to my financial horror, my two roommates both got engaged and moved out on me. That meant I was stuck with a four-bedroom apartment and nine months left on the lease. I was barely making my own rent when my roommate Alyssa told me that her younger brother was looking for a place to stay and, if I didn't mind sharing the place with a man, he would like to have her room. Ha! Was she kidding? I would have shared the apartment with Charles Manson if he could come up with his part of the rent.

And Fredrico, my roommate's brother, and I lived together pretty amiably for about a month. Then he said that his friend, Kevin, was also looking for a place and asked if he could move into one of the empty bedrooms.

"Does Kevin have a job?" I asked him.

"He's a physical therapist."

"Hell yeah," I told him. "He can move in tonight."

But that was two months ago. And now I didn't like living with two men so much. Sure they were good for the things that go bump in the night, but they were messy and they ate too much and they were always telling my dates that I wasn't home or that I was talking to my fourth baby's daddy on the phone or that I was having a sex change operation. I looked around my messy apartment and blew my breath hard, filling up my cheeks with air, and buckled down onto the couch.

"Damn," I whispered, frustrated and tired. Harry had cut back hours once again so that I was down to fifteen hours a week. That wasn't going to do. I had thought about being a cocktail waitress at the strip club on Delancey Street, but I didn't want to be mauled by a bunch of horny guys every night. I could have actually gotten a job in my major, accounting, but I really wanted my days free to audition. I guess I could work at UPS, I thought. That was when Kevin came in the door.

Kevin was sharp. Even though he worked mostly with kids and old people, he dressed impeccably. He said that he always wanted to make a strong presentation, and he did. He was tall and muscular, and his skin was red like the color of cedarwood. He smelled like Joop! from his head to his feet, even when he came back from playing basketball. He had grown his soft, wavy hair into dreadlocks that hung to his shoulders. And I secretly thought he was fine but, being roommates, I kept my thoughts to myself.

Fredrico was fine, too, although he was a little young, only twenty. He was Puerto Rican and sometimes, when he was angry, his accent would get really thick. I thought that was sexy when he wasn't angry with me. He was tall, too, and thin but with nice pectoral muscles and broad shoulders. He had a trim mustache, and he wore his hair close to his head. He looked mean and scary to people who didn't know him. But women adored him and literally followed him around trying to get to know him better. He was a nice guy, and he didn't date a lot. He kept saying he was going to grow up and marry me. He had been saying that since he was sixteen. I told him that his feet weren't big enough.

Kevin sat down on the couch next to me.

"What's wrong?" he asked.

"Broke. About to be dancing on tables. Tired of Fat Harry's ass always trying to jip me."

"I can dig it," he said. Then he patted my knee and got up to go into the kitchen. "You could always merry Rico," he joked.

I'd rather marry you, I thought. But I just sucked my teeth and rolled my eyes at him. He started laughing.

"You could be our house woman," he said.

"What the hell is a house woman? I'm already the house woman."

"No, you're not. You don't perform any duties."

"Okay," I said, knowing exactly where he was going with this. "What are a house woman's duties, Kevin?"

"Cook, clean, do laundry…give head."

I took one of the pillows off the sofa and beamed it at his nose. "I'm not having sex with either one of you funky clowns!" I yelled at him and hit him again in the back with my shoe. He ran upstairs laughing and locked his door.

A few days later, Rico and I lay on my bed flipping through a magazine and sharing a bag of hot potato chips.

"So, when we get married, are you going to quit this acting thing and stay at home and raise my babies?"

"Shut up, Rico."

We came to an ad for a hair product with two naked men sandwiching a woman between them. One was smelling her hair and the other one had his head pressed against her chest. "Be careful what you ask for," the ad read.

"Look at that," Rico pointed out. "That's us, me you and Kevin."

"In your nasty freak-boy dreams it is," I said and flipped the page.

"Why not?" he asked me. "You can't say you've never in your life thought about getting down with two men. If you say that then you're lying."

"Yeah, I've thought about it," I admitted. "But I'm not down with it. And it certainly wouldn't be with you two jerks."

"Why not?" he asked.

"Because you're jerks. And you live here," I told him. They weren't jerks really but I liked to tell them that. Especially when there were funky undershirts lying on the table in the living room or bags of Cheetos left by the toilet.

"No, I mean why wouldn't you do it at all?" he asked me trying to be serious.

"Well for one, I don't think it would turn out like this picture, that's for sure."

"What do you mean?"

"I mean, look at them. They're all into her like they really care about her. But it doesn't really happen like that. I've seen movies. It's violent. It's like stick it here and jam it up there and flip her and smack her, and I'm just not down."

"So, if it could be like this picture, you would do it?" He smiled.

"Get out of my room. You ask too many questions," I told him.

"You would do it," he said before he left. "I know you would."

That night I dreamed about Rico, Kevin and me. It was a blurry dream though, and they were both kissing my legs when I woke up, so I never really got to the good part. But in the morning, my panties were creamy and sticking to me. The guys had turned me on. Even in my dreams, this was not a good idea.

The next Saturday night I had a date. And I was a little

excited about it, too. I had already cleaned the house and ironed my clothes, and my hair (which was fierce I might add) had already been whipped into shape earlier that day at the salon. I was going to be stunning for this guy, Thomas, who was also an actor, but a working one (unlike myself). I wanted to make a smooth first impression so I had to fix the guys dinner so that they would promise not to tell him anything weird about me when he came to the door.

"Just ask him to have a seat. That's all. Don't say anything else." I told them, and they sat on the couch smiling, promising and looking like liars.

I ran upstairs to take a shower. I put on the stereo and pulled out my favorite vanilla body wash. Then I stepped in the shower and lathered the scented gel onto my body. "Cassanova Brown" came on the radio, and I started to sing into my soap container. *My baby smiles, and always keeps me guessing...* I did the whole song and, since I was in the mood now for a concert, I also did a soulful acapella version of "A House Is Not a Home," before I realized I was supposed to be hurrying up. There was a knock at the door, and Rico peeked his head inside.

"Shelly," he said, "your date's downstairs. He looks like a buster."

"Shut up, Rico."

"You want me to wash your back?" he asked.

"Get out!" I told him. I heard the door close and lathered my own back as best I could. In a few seconds, though, I felt another set of soapy hands moving up and down my spine and across the top of my butt.

"I thought I told you to get out," I said.

"I'm just helping," he said, smiling coyly. "You have a pretty body. You have a very large butt, too. I like that."

"I'm gonna smack you in your head." I reached for the bottle of shower gel so I could hit him with it, and he grabbed my arm and spun me around. I slid into his arms.

"Gotcha," he said and kissed me on the mouth.

There are so few times in life we get to say "what the hell" and actually go with what we feel. I had really never had one of those times before. But his arms felt nice around my waist, and I didn't want to move away. I had one of those moments right then and there. *What the hell*, I thought. *He's cute. He's sweet. I'm horny, and my date is a buster.* And I kissed him back. I licked my tongue across his lips and then probed deep into his mouth, licking the roof and wrapping his own tongue around mine. He slid his soapy hands down to my butt and rubbed it in slow, sensual circles, gripping me every now and then, and then letting go. I reached down and pulled his shirt from over his head and unbuttoned his shorts so that they fell to the floor.

"Get in with me," I whispered, and he climbed into the shower. I poured the shower gel into my hands and lathered his hard, round chest. Then I swirled the suds around his stomach and moved my hands down to his groin. His manhood was terrific. Not at all what I had expected from such small feet. He wasn't hard yet, but his dick was heavy, filled with anticipation as it sat on my thigh like a hungry wolf waiting for its prey. It was pretty, too, and perfectly shaped. It was a little darker than the rest of his body and the head was fat. I took it in my hands and rubbed the warm, soapy lather over it slowly. It grew even mightier in my hand, and my nipples and clitoris stood on end.

Rico held my breasts in his hands and allowed the water to fall on them just enough to wash the soap off my nipples. Then he took them into his mouth one at a time. First, he slowly placed his lips on top of one nipple and moved his fat tongue over it, flicking it hard and then returning to soothe it with the same warm motion. He did the same thing to my other breast, making love to each of them individually as if they were whole people to be made love to. I leaned up against the shower wall, his long, fat manhood still throbbing in my soapy hand. He had dropped to his knees and was licking my navel and holding me by the hips when there was knock at the door.

"Shelly, this corny-ass dude is down here waiting...." Kevin stuck his head in the door. He could only see our shadows through the shower curtain. "What the..." he whipped open the shower curtain and started to smile. "Damn," he said. "It shoulda been me." And he turned to walk away. I reached out and grabbed his hand.

"Don't go," I told him.

This was the second time in my life I had said "What the hell," and I wasn't going to be sorry. I wanted him to stay. I wanted them both to stay.

His eyes got big, and a sly smirk came across his face. Rico moved downward and began to kiss the hair on my mound. He was digging into my thighs with his fingers, and it hurt, but I didn't want him to stop.

"Please don't go," I begged again. And Kevin took off his own shirt and shorts and got into the tub behind me. He started kissing my neck and shoulders, and Rico began rolling his tongue around my clitoris. I was wet from the inside out. Both of these strong, beautiful men...holding me...touching me so...softly. I had never envisioned it being like this. I always thought it would be some kind of violation, but it was sweet and soft and strong and intense. Kevin began to slide down, too, and he kissed my back and my butt, licking me up and down and nibbling on the soft parts of my skin. He spread open my cheeks and licked me from one end to the other, flattening his tongue and digging deep into holes. Rico worked the front of the area, still gripping my thighs. Then he came up. I was bent over, and Kevin took this opportunity to rub his heavy instrument between my legs. He was so hard, and I could feel his heat up against my butt and back and now pulsating against my labia. His manhood reached from behind me to well in front of me, sticking out like a giant cherry-wood sword between my legs.

"Go ahead, Daddy," I said. "Put it in." I could feel his heavy exhale on my neck just then. He slid back and aimed his hard tool straight for my waiting box. My walls were already pouring. Aaaagghh. It felt like I had finally been fed after years and years of starvation.

He put it in slowly, first just the tip, and then moved closer, inch by inch, to make sure that I could handle his mass. He felt so good inside me, and I came on him and down my own soapy legs. Yes, I was finally being fed, but I was not full. Rico was still in front of me with his swollen dick in his hands. He tapped it lightly up against my lips, and I stuck out my tongue and licked the opening. He closed his eyes and sighed a deeply. Then he guided it slowly into my mouth, and I tightened my cheeks around it. He moved to the back of my throat, and I slid my tongue over it in circles. I held my hands on the sides of the tub to brace myself for Kevin's impact. I wanted him to hit it and hit it hard. Rico guided his own stiffness inside my mouth, and I made it warm and wet and welcome. I let go of the sides of the tub and gripped his smooth butt up in my hands. I could smell his young horniness exuding from between his legs.

His newness to love, his excitement, smelled like young, sweet, funky, beautiful, passionate cum. And I was trying to suck away whatever was left of his innocence. From behind me, Kevin worked my insides slowly, occasionally ramming it hard and then moving away softly and gently. He wrapped his huge arms around the front of my body.

I took Rico's penis into my palms and slid my hand up and down the shaft quicker and quicker. I wanted him to cum. I wanted to taste his fresh, young juices. I took his penis out of my mouth only long enough to lick between his legs and check the tightness of his testicles. He was on the verge of explosion. His eyes fluttered. Kevin growled behind me. I came when he tightened his grip on my breasts, and my trembling caused Rico's penis to begin to throb. In the next instant I was swallowing a hot, salty soup, and he was falling to the floor of the tub on his knees. At the same time, Kevin pulled out and exploded all over my back. I came again, with the hot syrup trickling down my back and the warm cream dripping down my legs. Then I leaned back against Kevin's huge, hairy chest, and he wrapped his arms around me. Rico laid his head on my stomach and wrapped his arms around my legs. For the moment, they were loving me. It was all about me. And I was loving them.

I went downstairs, wrapped in my towel, my fierce hairstyle now drenched and clinging to my shoulders, only to find Thomas still sitting on the couch, eating Cheetos and watching TV.

"Oh, Thomas, I didn't know you were here. I'm going to have to take a rain check on that date. I'm a little tired right now," I said. I showed him out and went into the kitchen and got a gallon of iced tea and three plastic cups and ran back upstairs.

In my room, Kevin sat on the edge of the bed massaging his manhood back into form. Rico lay beneath the covers, his already hard dick making a small tent in the sheets. I smiled at them from the door and wondered, since I had cooked dinner and all, if I would be paying rent this month. Somehow I doubted it, and I climbed into bed with my roommates.

Pant

I had never been inside a store like Pant…if you could call it a store. The top floor was more like a gentlemen's club that had opened its membership to women. It was dark and crowded, and house and disco music played so loudly that I could feel the beat in my chest and groin. Barely dressed women rocked and gyrated on three different platforms and men and women alike cheered and screamed for them. There were dancers up there to suit everyone: tall, short, thick, thin, classic blonde, black as night. Each of them moved as if they had been born to move. They were not the type of girls who danced for the money. They were the type that liked to dance. They liked to climb on top of people and pretend to make love to them. They liked to bend over in front of people and finger the brightly colored thong between their cheeks. They enjoyed the look on people's faces. They liked shaking their ample breasts in front of men's eyes and waiting for them to develop the inevitable blank stare before their chins dropped and their mouths opened in an effort to take the breasts between their lips before the dancer pulled away smiling no. They enjoyed pretending to lick someone or suck someone or ram their make-pretend penises into someone's ass. They craved the bulge or moistness in people's pants just as much as their audience did. I liked these dancers. They were beautiful to me. I, who would never have balls big enough to climb on the stage or strut around the room naked twirling and smiling like a superstar, I admired these women. Envied them even. Exhaling a wishful sigh, Jeffrey pulled me out of my exotic reveries.

"You're all heated," he said, laughing at me when my eyes would get big at the sight of someone's breasts or disproportionately large behind. "You like this, don't you? And you're letting these women get you all heated up."

"Why would you bring me here," I asked him, "if you didn't want me to like it?"

A young woman, thin with round hips and full breasts, came and stood in front of us. She was a cinnamon-   colored girl with an islandlike tan, and she reminded me of summertime even though it was February. "I'm hot," she announced, taking an ice cube out of Jeffrey's glass. "Would you put this on me?" She handed the ice cube to me and I, somewhat hesitantly, began to rub it on her back and shoulders. She introduced herself as Carmen and rubbed her hands along my thighs as I moistened her back. Jeffrey watched us with his hand over his mouth as if he was in deep thought. He was smiling under there, I knew, and he was also getting hot. Carmen reached out and pulled a chair over to ours. She turned around and sat in the chair with her legs spread wide open, dangling her calves and feet over either arm.

I couldn't help but stare. She was wearing an orange G-string and the small triangle of fabric just barely covered what she needed it to cover. Her box looked fat and ripe inside her panties, and I blinked and looked away.

Then she reached in the glass and took another piece of ice. "Here," she said, handing me the second piece of ice. I reached for it but instead of letting it go, she held on to my hand. She guided it around her breasts and neck and down her stomach to her navel. Jeffrey squirmed in his seat trying to keep his penis from jumping through his zipper. We both stopped at the top of her orange triangle. That was enough playing lesbo for me. She smiled and wrapped her long legs around each other. "Don't forget to try Room Four before you go," she said and touched my face softly and strutted away.

"Yo," Jeffrey breathed, his lips dry from forgetting to close his mouth "I thought she was gonna let you finger her or something right there in the chair."

I thought she was, too. That's why I stopped. But I didn't say that to Jeffrey. He liked the idea of two girls having sex. Two guys, well that was something altogether different. But two girls, to him, that was the epitome of sexy. I had never been with another woman though. I wasn't really sure how I felt about that. And I wasn't about to finger a stripper in the middle of a club, no matter how riled up Jeff was.

The club was dark, and the only thing that lit the way were the fluorescent underwear on the dancers and the floor lighting to the exits. We walked out the back exit and down the stairs. It was not the way we came in and, at first, we started back the other way. Then a group of girls passed us on the stairs. They were all dressed in black and all holding dog leashes in their hands. They had on long, black wigs and looked very serious and menacing. Three feet behind them followed a large man attached by chains to their leashes. He was beet red and there were bruises on his thighs and chest but he was smiling. They disappeared into the darkness at the top of the stairs.

"Oh, keep going this way," Jeffrey pushed, wanting to see what else was going on down there. At the bottom of the stairs were three huge fish tanks. It was as if we had walked into the state aquarium. In the first tank there were two sharks. They were small for sharks, at least compared to the ones on TV, but they looked ominous enough, and they swam circles, one behind the other. In the last fish tank were two huge yellow and blue tropical fish. They must have been three feet long. And they, too, swam in circles one behind the other. And, as we passed, a dim light came on in the center tank, and we saw a flash of skin. I stopped and the light went out. When it came on again we saw two bodies, male and female. Then the light went out again. By the third time, we were hooked; reeled into the tank by curiosity. The lights came on brighter and flashed like violet strobe lights, allowing us to see the couple making love inside the tank. It was filled with pillows instead of water and, at the moment, she was on her knees with her palms pressed against the glass, and he was behind her ramming himself into her, making her bump her head periodically against the glass. I looked at her face . She was enjoying this beating she was taking. She made strange faces, pained and filled with ecstasy. She didn't care if people saw her either. She liked it. I couldn't remember if I had ever made faces like that. Maybe I had once. Maybe I had liked the feeling of a huge steel man inside of me at one time. But, if I had, it had been long ago and certainly not with Jeffrey. He was big, for sure. But he was clumsy inside me. He poked and jammed and finished early. We watched for as long as the lights were on but they went off before the couple changed position.

Then we walked farther into a lighted area. It was like the difference between Babylon and Barnes & Noble. It was almost clinical. There were shelves of books, thousands and thousands of books, many not even in English, all about making love: how to make love, how to achieve orgasm, the proper ways to perform oral sex, love stories, magazines, journals, More Sex, Sex and Self, Better Sex Through Fitness. There were at least ten aisles of sexual discourse, self-help and research. Then, in the front of the store by the door there was a large glass counter. Inside were the top-of-the-line vibrators, condoms, dildos, jellies, toys and herbal potency drinks. Behind it was a wall of costumes, shoes, whips, handcuffs and wigs. The woman that stood between the counter and the wall was holding a biology textbook with a University of Pennsylvania decal glued to the front. She was light brown with long brown-and-bleach-streaked hair. She was small at the top but thick through the thighs and buttocks. Her smile was a little off center, though instead of being a liability, it turned out charming. She was on the phone making a personal call. When she said "I love you, too" into the phone she made kissing noises into the receiver. Her lips were shaped like fat gold painted hearts. She hung up the phone and turned to us.

"Hi. I'm Charlotte. Can I help you with something? We have a huge selection of toys and aids, and anything you don't see we can order."

"No," Jeffrey said. "We're just about to go."

"Okay, well, come back and see us again," she said. Jeffrey turned to walk out of the store, and I turned with him then I turned back to the counter.

"I'm supposed to ask you about Room Four," I told her. One of her eyebrows raised by itself.

"Who told you to ask about Room Four?" she asked me.

"Carmen," I said. Then she smiled a broad, toothy smile. Her grin was devilish and coy but her eyes were warm. "Walk with me," she said and stepped out from behind the counter. Jeffrey started to follow but she stopped him. "Ladies only." She took my hand.

We walked down another hallway and stooped outside of a room whose entrance was surrounded by dressing screens decorated in dragons and naked Chinese ladies.

"What's Room Four?" I asked Charlotte.

"This is it. Room Four is for tryers," she answered.

"What kind of tryer?" I asked, getting nervous. "Trying what?"

"Room Four is for women only," she answered.

"Huh?"

29

"Well, you could try this." She pulled out a plastic butterfly and a remote control. "You attach this to your vagina with this strap," she said, holding the butterfly up. "Then your lover has control of this," she said, pointing to the remote. "So you could be in another room, or at a party or something, and he could be working you and not even be with you. It's a lot of fun. It's $59.99."

"Can I be at work and he be at home?" I asked.

"No. It only has a range of fifty feet," she told me.

I was only a little disappointed. "Actually," I said, "I'm looking for something a little less mechanical."

Her one eyebrow rose again. "Is it 'yet' yet?"

"Maybe," I said, blushing.

We walked back down the hallway to the entrance of the coveted room. I was nervous and anxious, and my stomach and legs felt jittery. Charlotte held my hand as we entered the room. Surprisingly there were about twenty other women inside. And it was a harem. It looked like the inside of a genie's bottle. Red and orange silk curtains hung from the rafters. Huge purple and red pillows covered the floors. There were lounge chairs and small tables. A waitress, dressed in a see-through orange gown with a veil over her nose and mouth walked around filling up glasses and serving fruit.

"The drinks cost. Everything else is free. You don't have to do whatever. You can do anything you want to," Charlotte said, still holding my hand. She squeezed it a little and I looked down. American manicure. I always did like that.

A small white woman with dark hair came over to me and grabbed my other hand.

"This is Macy," Charlotte said, introducing us. "This is her first time here, too. Macy this is…" She paused for a minute. "You never told me your name." She looked at me.

"Lisa," I lied.

"Well, Macy, this is Lisa. I'll leave you now." And then she turned and walked away.

"I just thought you were so pretty," Macy said, talking at a thousand miles per hour. "I've never done this before but I always like have freaky dreams about having sex with ladies and a lot of times they're Black ladies, and one of them looks just like you. You know, like your color and hair and everything. I just think you're beautiful. I just had to come over and tell you that."

Macy was pretty. Her body was tight and compact like a gymnast or a fitness instructor. Her hair stopped at her shoulders and was thick and black and shiny. She had a long, thin nose like maybe she was Italian.

"Thank you," I said.

"Well," she said. "Do you wanna do something?"

"Wow." I guess I had been expecting more along the lines of conversation. But this was not a chat room. It was what it was. I took a deep breath. "Um, sure."

We walked over to the darkest corner of the dimly lit room. She stared at me for the longest time once we got there. It was disconcerting to be looked at so longingly by someone I didn't know. I turned her around gently by her shoulders so that her back was facing me. She had on a button-up shirt, and I began to unbutton it slowly. Her breasts were full for someone as tightly built as she was, and her nipples were long and hard. From behind her, I cupped them softly in my hands, and she let her head fall back onto my chest. I squeezed her breasts gently, massaging my finger lightly over her nipples, and she moaned.

"Oh, Lisa. I think I am going to like you too much."

I stopped for a second because I forgot who Lisa was, but she didn't notice. She had latched her lips onto my neck and was kissing me back and forth between my chin and my shoulders. Then I moved my hands down toward her skirt. There was only one button, and the skirt dropped to her feet as if I had thrown down a flag. She was wearing black thong panties with double hip straps. I had the same ones at home. I had bought them from Victoria's Secret when I first met Jeffrey. I hadn't taken them out of the box yet.

She bent over in front of me and took them off. When she turned around she began to unbutton my blouse. I was still in my work clothes: a corporate shirt, slacks and pantyhose. No. That would take too long. I didn't want to be naked. I didn't want to be making love. I just wanted to see. I stopped her and sat her down on one of the pillows. She started to giggle. I knelt in front of her and spread her legs.

"Oh my god!" she screamed loudly. I hadn't done anything yet. "That's Rebecca over there. Hi, Beck!"

What the hell? I thought. *Is she actually talking to someone else?*

"We don't have to do this," I told her.

"No. Yes, we do. I'm sorry. It's just that my girlfriend just walked in. And I can't believe it. She's such a prude. But let's go."

I kissed her thigh and worked my way closer to the middle. I didn't like this. I didn't like her. She smelled like bologna and between her legs smelled like some other type of processed pork.

"You know what, I'm not feeling this," I said. "Let's stop."

Another woman was behind the counter when I stepped out into the store. As I walked toward the door, someone tapped me on the back.

"Are you leaving?" Charlotte asked me. "How was it?"

"I didn't...Well, I...It just wasn't right, you know. I didn't like her. She smelled like lunch meat. She was silly. It just didn't feel right, so I left."

"If it doesn't feel right," Charlotte said, taking my hand into her own again, "it's not right."

"Thanks," I said and started to walk out again.

"You know," she said to me, "I know your real name isn't Lisa."

I turned around and smiled at her. "It's Marisol," I told her.

"Marisol. That's pretty. Are you Spanish?"

"Just my dad," I said.

"That's cool. Well, Marisol, you could go or," she paused, "you could come with me."

"No," I said. "Not another roomful of strangers."

"No," she said, still holding on to my hand. "Just me."

We went through another door and climbed another set of stairs. She unlocked the door to an office. It was her office, her name on the desk, pictures of her and her kids on the wall.

She poured us two cups of orange tea, and we sat on a futon and talked. I liked her. She was nice. She was pretty. She used her warm, heavy voice to say things to me. She told me that she never let people come up here but that she had a good feeling about me. And intuition, after all, is better than facts. I felt relaxed around her, and I sat back in my chair and laid my head back against the pillows. She stood and walked around to the back of the chair. Then she put her hands on my shoulders and started to massage my neck. It felt so good. Jeffrey was so rough and thumby. His massages always felt like I was being poked or kneaded like a piece of dough. My shoulders melted. She bent down and unbuttoned my blouse. Then she massaged my breasts through my bra. Gentle, firm squeezes and light touches on the nipples. Before I realized it, my bra was off, and she was in front of me. When I opened my eyes, she tilted my head up and kissed me very tenderly on the lips. I put my hand to the back of her head and kissed her again, this time sliding my tongue between her lips and into her mouth. Her mouth was still warm from the tea and something between my legs woke up and did a dance inside my womb.

I stood up, and she removed my pants and pantyhose and underwear in one fell swoop. Then she wrapped her arms around me and pressed her small, perky breasts against mine. She kissed my neck. I closed my eyes again. She bent her knees and began to sink lower, taking one of breasts into her mouth. She licked around my nipple at first and then spread her tongue out to encompass even more of the area. Then she opened her mouth even wider and shoved my entire breast inside and slid back off it, tugging and sucking on the nipple as though she were an infant. Her hands moved around the rest of my body like a masseuse. She let go of my right breast to give attention to the left. Her hands were between my legs, and I was a little embarrassed at the puddle collecting there on her wrist. She pushed me down onto the futon and spread my legs. I opened my eyes and looked at her, and she smiled at me.

"It's okay," she told me and licked the shiny juice off her hand. She took my foot into her hand and massaged it slightly and then kissed and bit the arch. I shivered. Then she kissed my ankles and licked my calves and knees. She kissed my inner thighs and moved her tongue in circles around my thighs and up to my pelvis and navel.

I was so wet. I thought I was going to scream if somebody didn't stick something up inside me and really quick. And just when I was going to bust, she opened her mouth and placed it over my clitoris and stated to hum. *Hmmm.* I almost hit the ceiling. Then I started to hum. (*Oh what a beautiful morning, oh what a beautiful day*) And I grabbed her hair and pulled it, pushing her face deeper into me. She grabbed my butt with both hands and licked the opening to my box, sucking up all the juices that had been drenching her hands and chin. Then she stuck out her tongue and licked my lips, spreading them apart and pushing them back together with the tips of her fingers. She nibbled gently on my clitoris and then flicked her tongue fast against the outside of my vagina, and I came, a tiny river of milky jism spilling out.

I think that my orgasm must have turned her on because, after that, she drove her tongue straight up inside me and pulled my hips toward her face. I moved them back, and she pulled them forward again. And again. And, in a moment, she had stopped pulling me, and I was rocking back and forth of my own volition, allowing her long, fat tongue to move in and out and in and out of me. I never let go of her hair. I was loving every second of what she was doing. She rode me with her mouth for what seemed like hours. Then she raised up and jammed her middle finger inside me...hard. She circled it a little and lifted me up by my box. Then she jammed it in again and again, and I came again and again.

I screamed like I was a virgin. And, in truth, at least to this kind of lovemaking, I was. And when she finally pulled away from me, I collapsed over my knees. When I looked up again she was standing over me smiling.

Man or no man, I had never cum that many times in my life. She dropped her skirt, and her shaved pussy stared me right in the face. She straddled me in the chair and rubbed herself up against me, her mound grinding up against mine, making a pool of mixed pleasures in the crevices of the cushion. I held on to her butt with both hands, spreading her cheeks wide, allowing her to press against me harder. She moved on top of me like the wind moves. Gently at first and then in gust of energy that surprises you into action. I thought that maybe I would pass out. I wanted to screw her forever. It would have been okay if we never stopped except that I would have died of overstimulation or electrocution or something.

I pushed her up by her butt so that her crotch was in front of my face. It was beautiful, and she smelled sweet. A natural, human sweet. I could feel the heat from within her on my chin, and I could feel her pussy pulsating, waiting for me to touch it. She dripped a creamy sauce onto my nose. I didn't hesitate. I stuck my tongue dead in the center of her softness, and she exhaled and came all over my face. I lapped it up, licking the outside of her lips and moving my mouth back and forth between her butt and her clit. She moved in circles on my face, and I loved it. I ate her well into the night. She tasted like a mixture of sweetness and salt that reminded me of chocolate-covered pretzels. I took all that I could away with me the next morning when I left.

Jeffrey asked me where I had been, and I told him that I was in Room Four telling all the other women how big his dick was. He believed me and encouraged me to go back more often. That way, after listening to them gripe, I would be grateful for his sexual prowess and unconventionally large manhood. And I took Jeffrey's advice. I did go back...as often as I could.

Loving for Life

I knew my husband even before I knew myself. He was my older brother's best friend. My mother says that when she was pregnant, he used to listen to her stomach all the time and talk into her navel about the terrors of preschool, what happens when you play with matches and the differences between The Incredible Hulk and Shazaam. He was at our house so much when we were young that it was a wonder that I never thought of him as a brother, too. But, even at three and four, I never did. I thought he was beautiful and amazing and talented. And my brother was retarded and silly and dirty and mean.

But, by then, of course Will had no interest in me. I was little and didn't know how to do anything. If I ran, I fell. If he threw something to me, I let it hit me in the face. If I laughed too hard, I peed on myself. William and my brother, Tony, alike, were disgusted by my ineptness. That is, until the seventh grade when I grew almost eight inches taller and three cup sizes bigger in the front.

Of course Tony still found me utterly repulsive, but William began to be a whole lot more interested in me and my life. All of a sudden he wanted to know why I was hanging out here and what I was doing there. He became a weird combination of friend, boyfriend, security guard. For a while it made me sick. Every time I thought a guy was cute, he shot him down, or told him to go the hell home, or talked so badly about the poor boy that I was embarrassed to bring him to the house.

"Oh, he only does that because he likes you. He just doesn't want you to be with anyone else," My mother would say laughing. But to me it was a far cry from funny. It was awful. And it kept me a virgin far longer than I wanted to be.

Eventually, William got cute to me. His goofy smile turned charming, and he let his short, frizzy hair (that always made him look like baby chick) grow into a nice curly bush. He picked up a little weight and grew a few inches taller and, all of a sudden, I was chasing girls away from him instead of the other way around.

"Look here, girl," he said to me one day. "I don't understand you. You don't want to be with me…".

"Yeah," I said with my twenty-year-old hand on my hip.

"But you don't want anyone else to be with me."

"So?"

"So, if you don't want to play, why you keep messing up the game?"

"Maybe I do want to play," I said to him. It was August, and it was nasty hot outside and had been for days. Even in what should have been the cool of the evening we were sweating just sitting there on the steps. William's shoulders were shining, and I imagined that his whole body would be glistening, all muscular and strong and perfect. There were beads of sweat sliding slowly down my chest, and he traced one with his finger to the tip of my neckline.

"Forget it," he said to me. "You're not ready."

"Oh, yes, I am," I told him, trying to sound cool and womanly and seductive, but he wasn't buying it.

"I know you," he told me. "I'll know when you're ready."

He spent the entire fall running from me. Every chance I got to get close to him, I did. I danced with him at every party, always parting my legs ever so slightly on the slow songs. I hugged him tighter than I should have every time I saw him on the street. I called him every week with something to fix: the car, the TV, the hot-water heater. And every time he bent over to repair the thing, I made sure I was standing there with my breasts or my pussy or my freshly glossed lips right in his face.

My mother noticed it once when we were in the kitchen, and I purposely dropped the ice right in front of him. I was wearing tight black jeans and a cropped sweater. I bent over in slow motion, picking the ice cubes off the floor one by one. He tried not to stare at my butt while my mother was standing there but I made it damn near impossible.

"Reagan, get your fresh, fast ass upstairs and out of Will's face!" she yelled, swinging at me with the dustpan. I ran upstairs. Sure it worked for a minute. One minute exactly. But I was on a mission. I was tired of being a virgin. I felt like an animal. I was practically in heat. I went to bed thinking about William and me making love, and my pussy throbbed from loneliness every night. Every morning I woke up with the sheets balled up and tucked between my legs, only to find that I had flooded my panties with midnight orgasms. I was ready. I was beyond ready. And he was playing games.

By Christmas I had begun to lose hope. I didn't want to have sex with anyone else, and William was not relinquishing the goods. We always had a big Christmas dinner, and half of the neighborhood ate at our house. On Christmas Eve, my mother sent me to the market because she had run out of mayonnaise and she was trying to make potato salad.

"Can you take me to the store?" I called William and asked.

"No problem," he said. I could not then, nor can I now, remember him ever telling me no—except for sex. All my life, he had been there when I needed him. When someone snatched my earrings on the train, it was he who picked me up and drove me to school for the rest of the year. It was he who found out that it was a crack addict named Bony Nate who had taken them, then he beat up Nate and bought me some new earrings for my birthday.

It was William who had explained to me about things like sex and love and AIDS and how to tell knockoff jeans from designers. He was the one that taught me to listen for the jazz riffs in hip-hop songs and how to pop a clutch and what, exactly, was a punt return. Of course he would drive me to the supermarket on Christmas Eve.

The market was closed. In fact, every market was closed. So we wound up getting five really small jars of mayonnaise from the 7-Eleven. When he finally parked the car back in front of the house, I reached my arm over to his side and slid in front of him.

"I want you to make love to me," I said. "I'm ready. I've been ready. Aren't you?"

He smiled briefly and then looked at me. His eyes got serious, and his lips twisted up. "Why?" he asked me. "Why me?"

Oh, hell. Why? What was this, Twenty Questions?

"Duh!" I was highly upset. "I mean if you have to ask…"

"You should do it with someone you love, Reagan," he said. "Do you love me?"

Of course I loved him. What type of stupid-ass question was that. But couldn't we just screw? Did it have to be so deep?

"Of course I love you," I answered. "Of course I do."

He pulled away from the curb and then parked again five houses down in front of his own garage. He opened the door to my side of the car and led me by the hand through the basement entrance and into his room. I had been here a thousand times. It was no different. And yet, it was all new. It smelled like him, like his cologne, his soap, his sweat. His sheets smelled like the sheets I had been dreaming of and woke up clinging to. The walls were soothing to me. The carpet felt fresh and springy under my feet. He turned on the stereo. I sat down on his bed.

"You love me?" Will asked again. He took off his shirt and his strong, muscular chest puffed up in front of my eyes. He must have had a ten-pack of ab muscles, and I counted them all the way down to the belt on his jeans.

"Sure I love you," I said, licking my lips. Either it was me, or he was getting finer by the second.

"Do you trust me?" he asked.

"Of course I do," I said, taking off my sweater. I got a chill, and my nipples hardened. I closed my legs to keep from exploding.

"Then lay back," he told me, and I did.

He unbuttoned my jeans and slid them down over my hips and tossed them onto the floor. He placed my hands above my head and straddled my legs. I looked up at him, and he smiled.

"You don't know how long I've waited for you to be mine," he said. I blushed but I didn't say anything. It wasn't meant for me to say anything. He bent down and kissed me on the lips. He had full, hot lips, and they seemed to ignite my own. He opened my mouth with his tongue and licked the inside of my top lip and across my teeth. Then he swirled his tongue around mine and pulled away, gently sucking on my bottom lip. He kissed my chin and then my chest. He kissed around the lace on my bra and traced my nipples with his finger. My breathing went from slightly more rapid than usual to an all-out pant like a dog. Then he kissed his way down to my stomach. His mustache tickled me but I didn't laugh. When he got to my panties, he licked across my stomach, tracing the red lace with his tongue. I was ready, but I wasn't all the way ready. The White girls I went to school with had been giving and receiving head since the seventh grade. That was something they did like kissing. It came as a prerequisite to sex. But the Black girls, we learned it all in reverse. Giving head was like advanced sex. It was more special than sex. And since his mouth was kissing the outside of my panties, I could only assume what was next. But I was too turned on to be afraid. And it was Will. Why would I ever be afraid? He spread my legs apart and sat down on the floor between them. He put his mouth over my crotch and licked the opening to my pussy right through my panties. It was such a weird hot sensation; I started to drip right away. Then, with his forefinger, he pulled my panties away from me and stuck his tongue in between my legs. He licked my clit several times, and I moaned. I almost yelled but it just wouldn't come out.

"You like that?" he asked. I didn't answer him.

"I said, do you like that?" His tone changed, and I opened my eyes. He stood, and he was holding a piece of wire clothesline in his hands. I started to move but I realized that my feet were tied to the bottom of the bed.

"Will! What are you…" I started to yell at him but he put his hand over my mouth.

"You said you trusted me," he said. "I won't do anything you don't like. Okay?"

I nodded, and he let go of my mouth.

"But…"

"Shhh," he hushed me again; this time with just his finger. Then he dropped back down to his knees. He couldn't get my panties off with my legs tied apart so he tore them off me. They were brand-new Christmas panties, and I was mad, but only for an instant. He immediately calmed me, gracing me with his warm mouth, sliding it slowly over my pussy, letting me feel his hot breath and anticipate his long, wet tongue. Then he stuck his tongue out and licked my clit again lightly. He rubbed the lips of my box together with his fingers, and they slid around easily in my juices. Then he took his tongue as far to the rear as he could reach and then pressed it up against me as hard as he could, dragging it slowly up toward my waiting entrance. When he finally hit the spot, I howled and tears came to my eyes. He sucked on my lips lightly at first and then he tugged on them with his tongue and teeth firmly and, when he stopped, he dug his tongue deep inside of me and kept it there for a moment while I quivered over and over. Then he stiffened it and moved it around in big, fat circles inside of me. I was about to bust. The Black girls in my dorm didn't know what they were missing a little bit. White people always keeping secrets, I thought. At that moment, he opened his whole mouth wide and placed it over my entire pussy from the top of my mound almost to my asshole and began to hum and suck and lick and hum some more. "Oh!" I found myself saying over and over. I wasn't trying to say anything. It just kept spilling out.

He rammed his tongue into me and then pulled on my hips. I wasn't sure what he wanted but I knew I didn't want him to stop. He pulled his tongue away and then rammed it in again, again pulling my hips toward his face.

"Do you know how to fuck, Rey? Do you know how to move those juicy hips of yours?"

"Yes," I said.

"Then bring 'em to me," he said. "Fuck me. Fuck my tongue."

Oh…my…goodness! I was going to die. Right there, right at that moment. That was so freaky. But I liked it. I moved my hips forward to meet his mouth. After a few thrusts, I grabbed his hair and pulled it, guiding him into me. I moved my hips around in circles, and he held my butt in his hands. I could feel his chin digging into my pussy, and it felt good, hard and solid. If his chin felt like this, I could only imagine what the real thing would be like. He flattened his long tongue and sucked up all the juices around my box and then stood up and dropped his jeans.

Will was not the type of guy to talk about his dick, but he could have given a sister some warning. It was huge. It was big and fat and purple and shiny. It was the most beautiful thing I had ever seen. I wanted it in me so badly that I came just look-

ing at its massiveness. But I knew that there was no way in hell
that it would ever fit. He held it in his hand and stroked it
slowly. My mouth fell open.

"Do you want this?" he asked. "Is this what you've been begging me for all this time?"

"Yes," I whimpered. But what was I supposed to do with it?
My pussy was not that big.

"Touch it," he told me. "Sit up and touch it."

I sat up and reached for it with both hands. I held the base
of it firmly with my left while I stroked it up and down with my
right. His balls hung low behind it, and I wondered what was
the purpose of such huge balls anyway.

He took his dick in his own hands and then slapped it lightly across my cheek. Then he did it again.

"Taste it," he told me. "You wanted it so bad. See what it
tastes like."

I took his giant shaft back into my hands and licked the tip
of it quickly and softly. I figured that would be enough. I could
get away with that, and he wouldn't make me do it. But to my
own surprise, I liked the way it tasted. I liked the way it felt up
against my mouth. I even took it and slapped it up against my
own cheek. I parted my lips wide as wide I could manage and
swallowed the head of his commanding manhood into my
mouth. He put his hands in my hair and gently brought my face
closer to him. He was too big and filled my whole mouth without being even halfway in, but I licked around the fatness and
sucked on everything I could manage to hold. He groaned from
above me, and I could feel his balls tightening down by my chin.
He smelled so good. And he tasted so good. I was angry that
he had made me wait as long as he did. Then, just when I was
able to relax my throat enough to envelop him fully, he pulled
away and pushed me back down on the bed.

He laid his diamond-hard dick up against my throbbing
pussy. I was even wetter now; sloppy, messy wet. Holding his

big manhood in my mouth had triggered a juice box, and I couldn't stop the gush if I had tried.

He rubbed his dick around it now in circles, allowing me to feel his hardness, helping me to appreciate the sheer power I was going to be engulfing in my walls. He put the head of his dick at my entrance and pressed forward. I yelled. It felt like my insides were caving in. "Get out," I whined. "Get out of me."

"No," he said, stroking my hair with his fingers. "Not yet." He pressed farther still, and I clenched my butt cheeks and tried to push him away but he kept going. I held my breath and something snapped. "Oh shit!" I yelled.

"That's it, baby," he said, kissing me. "It's all good from here on out." And he was right. He went farther up into me, and my body relaxed to receive him. He worked slowly, understanding that he was a big man and I was new to love. He moved his hips in tiny circles and made small waves with his body. I rose to meet him whenever I could, and when I couldn't I just allowed him to live inside me. He felt good there, and I wanted him to stay inside me till the New Year came in. Then he started really moving. He backed up farther and slammed into me hard, and I yelled. He did it again, and I yelled again. Then he covered my mouth with his hands.

"This is it, right? This is what you wanted. So take it. Take this dick. Take it all."

Beneath his palms, I was screaming bloody murder. It hurt so much and, at the same time, I was cumming like the nine o' clock train. He rammed his huge dick into my newly inducted pussy, and I cried and I came all at the same time. I beat on his back with my fists but he ignored me, kissing me and telling me that it was my dick. That it had always been my dick. And that my pussy belonged to him, had always belonged to him and would always be his. He moved faster and faster, and soon I was not able to keep up, and my walls were about to collapse. He pressed in as far as he could go, took a deep breath and came out, dripping his white sauce all over my stomach and legs. I wrapped my arms around him. I couldn't have let him go if I wanted to. And I never wanted to.

"I love you, Reagan," he said. "I've just been waiting for you to love me back."

And I did love him. Every inch of him. Still do love him. Always will. Only, once again, the tables have turned…and now I get to tie his feet to the bed.

Pink

My best friend, Tasha, and I met because we both have an appreciation for the finer things. I was coming out of the post office, minding my own business and there, standing not five feet away from me, was the most gorgeous man with the most beautiful pair of legs I had ever seen. He was about six feet two and chestnut brown, with a mass of thick, curly hair and a goatee. He was dressed in a Sixers basketball short set, you know, with the tank top and the long shorts, and he had calves that were out of this world. And as he walked, his jersey and shorts swayed and clung to him, revealing that the upper part of his legs and the rest of his body, would be no less perfect. I couldn't move. I just stood there on the post office steps staring at the man's legs go by and his firm, muscular butt as he walked away from me. When I finally looked up I was locking eyes with another woman who, just like me, was just waking up from her Sixers man daze, and we both burst out laughing at each other's pure lack of dignity.

I liked her from the first day I met her. She was the total opposite of me. Tasha took everything so easily. She was open and artsy and silly and fun. And, even at twenty-seven, it had been a long time since I had just had fun. She was a professional woman like myself. She worked as an art director at an advertising agency. But unlike myself, an account manager at Boyden and Noble, a stock brokerage firm, she never let her job stress her out. It was like she didn't need her job even though I knew she didn't make half of what I was making, and she had just as many bills.

"He told us what he wanted us to do with this campaign," she said to me one day, casually talking about work. "And then he asked us if we thought it was hot. Did we think it would fly? I told him yeah it would fly just like a chicken."

"But chickens don't fly," I reminded her.

"That's what he said," she said, still talking about her boss. "And I said exactly what I mean. It's bullshit."

"You told your boss his idea was bullshit?" If I ever did that, I would be standing outside of Boyden with a "will work for food" sign and a tin cup. But I didn't have the balls she did.

"Yeah, Monica. You know, if I did half of the work he asked me to, I would never be able to get work in this town again. Even if it's his crappy idea, it's my design. It's part of my portfolio. I can't have people thinking I make crap like that."

"I would be fired. I would be so fired," I told her. "Go ahead."

"Well," she continued. "Then he says, it may be crap, but it has wings. And I said, you know, Merv, just because you add wings to bullshit, doesn't make it a good campaign. It makes it flying crap."

Tasha, despite company policy, went to work in jeans, tight hand-painted shirts and boots straight from 1972. Her hair was wild and curly and all over her head. She was a little too loud sometimes. And when she laughed, she was really laughing; not those fake ha-has and tee-hees people get after they grow up. I know she envied me a little because I had more money and I knew more people with more money. But I envied her smile, because it was always there and always real; nothing fake about it.

We had equally opposite relationship dramas as well. I was already divorced for one. That whole escapade was a bad accident straight out of high school. I got married to a military man who turned out to be some type of Black Nazi and who had to have his dinner served promptly at six or else I would promptly be getting my ass kicked. It lasted all of three months, and I packed my bags and went off to college.

Now, nine years later, I was living with Barry. He was cute and nice and financially stable and goal-oriented. I loved him. But having sex with Barry was like eating vegetables, good enough to sustain you, but not exactly chocolate chip cheesecake, if you know what I mean. I wasn't in love with him. I just loved him. There's a difference.

Tasha, though, had never married, and, from what I could tell, never intended to. She shared an apartment with her sister Rhonda and two men. (One of whom was her ex-boyfriend and the other one was her gay cousin, Marcellus.) It was a weird arrangement to me. But they were all like Tasha, an apartment full of loud, crazy people who never slept and didn't think it odd that the only things in their refrigerator were Slim Fast, beer and nacho dip.

Tasha's boyfriend, Basil, was completely in love with her. And she was completely in love with having sex with him. Again, there is difference.

I knew she didn't love him when she started giving me descriptions of his passion parts in graphic detail.

"I mean, it's big. Not like incredibly huge where you spend the whole time scooting back. But somewhere between big enough and too big. And it's pretty, too."

"Shut up, Tasha."

"I'm not lying. It's smooth all the way around, and it's practically the same color from the base to the tip. You know how some guys are all multicolored and what not?"

"No," I answered. "I've never seen a multicolored dick."

"You know what I mean. I mean, I even asked him, the first time, if he put makeup on it or skin toner or something."

"You are too stupid." I giggled. It took Tasha to ask a man if he put skin toner on his penis. That's what I meant. She was open. She made me laugh.

"What are you doing tonight?" she asked.

"Nothing," I said, knowing that Barry would be engulfed in the television and I would probably be finishing off the double chocolate Milanos and giving myself a pedicure.

"Me and Rhonda and Marcellus are going to the club. You wanna go?"

"What club?"

" Amethyst," she answered.

"Isn't that a gay club?" I asked. I didn't know about going to any Amethyst.

"It's whatever," she said, flagging her hand away. "I mean, there are a lot of gay guys there. They do drag shows and stuff. But there's a lot of straight people there, too. I always have fun. I mean, it's not the type of place you go looking for a husband. It's just fun."

Eventually she talked me into it. And, to tell the truth, I was kind of angry with myself that I had to be talked into having fun. I felt like I was getting old or something. So I made up for it by putting the shortest dress I had together with the boots with the highest heel.

"Where are you going?" Barry asked me as I was putting the finishing touches on my face. I had switched from my daytime bronze lip gloss to a velvety red shimmer stick that was working wonders with my outfit. With two more strokes of the magic mascara wand, I would be, as all divas say: "Fierce!"

"To the club with Tasha," I said casually.

"Oh. I thought we could stay in tonight and chill."

"Barry..." Didn't he know I was sick and damned tired of chilling? "No. You relax if you need to. I wanna go out."

"But, why?"

"Why?" You see what I was up against? And I was turning into him, slowly but surely. A little old man and his little old woman sitting on the couch forever chilling until they died. "I just wanna have some fun, Barry. Remember fun?"

When I got to the club Tasha met me in the lobby. She was in jeans, as usual, but with a tight, white halter top and her hair was blown out straight and laying on her shoulders. She looked great, and so did I, so we created a little commotion among the straight and bisexual men at the front door.

"Girl, you look amazing. That's all you needed was a little red in your life."

I hit the dance floor with Marcellus but he came at me with one high kick too many so I sat down and let him dance alone.

"Can I buy you another drink?" a deep voiced asked from behind me. When I turned around I almost choked on my maraschino cherry. It was the Sixers man from in front of the post office. Tasha and I had staked out that post office for months just trying to get a glimpse of the man again, and here he was, standing right in front of me in Amethyst of all places. Should have known, I thought.

"How about Sex on the Beach?" he asked.

"Moving a little fast there aren't you, Sheriff?" I said.

He smiled. "The drink. It's fruity. You'll like it." He ordered the drinks and then sat down across from me.

"Did you want to dance?" I asked him.

"No."

"Well, what brings you to my table?" I wasn't used to this scene, you know, with the games and all. At work I could play with the best of them. But, in real life, people should just come out and say what they want.

"Well," he said. "I think you're pretty." He paused. "And my girlfriend thinks you're pretty." My eyes widened; he paused again. "And we want to know if you want to come home with us."

Say what? I dropped my glass on the table and the ice slid into his lap.

"I'm so sorry," I said, unconsciously starting to wipe between his legs with my napkin. "You just caught me off guard."

"It's okay," he said. "So is that a yes or a no."

"No. No, no, no. I'm not here for... I mean I've never, well, I, uh...No, thank you. But I appreciate you asking." I started to run. My brain was headed for the door but my feet were still in the same place.

"Well look," he said, standing up and forcing me to come face-to-face with two huge mounds of pectoral muscle. "If you ever think you might change your mind, here's my number." He handed me his card, kissed me on the cheek (I guess to calm my racing heart) and then walked away. On the other side of the club I saw him lock arms with another woman. His girlfriend, I assumed. She was pretty. And I was glad to see that at least... I looked at the card: Jameson Hill, Personal Trainer...At least good ol' Jameson from the post office with the pretty legs wasn't gay after all.

When we left the club, we went back to Tasha's, and I told her all about Jameson and his girlfriend.

"Why'd you say no?" she asked me.

"What? Are you crazy?"

"That's still being voted on. But I'm just curious to know why you turned him down."

"Because I've never...well, I don't even know him for one. And I don't get down like that."

"Oh. So are you saying that you would have if you knew him?"

"I'm saying that that's just not my thing."

"You are so white bread. How do you know if you've never tried it?"

"Have you tried it?"

"Once or twice," she said. I wanted to be shocked but somehow I just wasn't.

"You liked it?"

"I loved it."

"Oh."

"As a matter of fact," she said, sitting down in the chair in front of me, "Basil and I were going to ask you if you would sleep with us."

"Are you for real?" If she had stood up she would have been stepping on my bottom lip. Now I was shocked! " Me? What?"

"Yeah." She said this softly, not in her usual loud, aggressive Tasha tone. "You are one of the most beautiful women we know. I mean, I've always thought you were hot, and Basil worships you. He thinks you have the greatest butt in the world."

I didn't know what to do. And I couldn't believe that I wasn't flipping out or insulted or running for my life. Actually, I was flattered.

"That's all good but I make it a point not to sleep with my friends' men."

"It doesn't count if I'm there, too." She smiled.

The doorbell rang, and she touched my cheek lightly before she ran to get it. When she came back in the room Basil was behind her.

"Speak of the devil," I said.

"We were just talking about you," she told him. "Well actually you and me and Monica."

"What about us?" he asked. Basil was lightweight fine, too. He was tall and light skinned with full, masculine lips. He wore his hair in braids and, like Tasha, was always in jeans and boots. He looked like a thug and, even though he had a degree in environmental engineering and a management job at OSHA, he still possessed some of his thuggish, roguish nature. He was built well with broad shoulders and a slim waist. And, when I saw him, I remembered Tasha's stories about how pretty his dick was, and I started to blush.

Tasha came and stood behind me and wrapped her arms around me. "About us getting together," she said. "All of us. I told Monica how fine we both thought she was. I'm just trying to get her to try something new."

"Oh." Basil smiled and took off his jacket.

"So, Monica, what do you think?" Now he sat down in front of me. Looking back I know that if I had not had those six or seven drinks at the club, I probably would have said good night right then. But, to tell the truth, Tasha's arms felt good around me. And when Basil sat down I could smell his cologne and his sweat, and I didn't want to leave. I didn't want to think. I felt good where I was.

He lifted my legs off the ground and put them in his lap. He took off his T-shirt. His chest and stomach were chiseled beyond my imagining. Then he took off my boots and began to rub my feet. From behind me, Tasha began to massage my shoulders. I closed my eyes and did not realize for a while that she had started kissing me between rubs on my neck and back. Basil slid his hands up my dress and pulled off my stockings. Then he knelt down on the floor in front of me.

"Don't be afraid," I heard Tasha say somewhere in the distance. "Just do what you feel. If you don't feel it, don't do it."

Basil continued to massage my feet and legs, only now he was working his way upward, kneading my thighs and hips. Tasha was still behind me, and she worked her way downward to my lower back. She slipped my dress up over my head, unhooked my bra and began to kiss me tenderly all over my back. I put my hands in Basil's hair and fingered his soft braids. He laid his head down in my lap and took a deep breath. I knew that he was smelling me, trying to gauge how sweet I was going to taste. Then he reached up and pulled my thongs down over my hips. Tasha made her way in front of me and then gently pushed me down on the bed. She touched my face lightly and then bent over to kiss me. Her mouth was soft and sweet and tasted like maraschino cherries. I had never kissed another woman, but, as she wrapped her tongue around mine, I forgot about what we were and just enjoyed that we were.

She moved down and began to massage my breasts in her small hands. It was a different kind of touch. Soft, but firm, and then she placed one of my nipples in her mouth, and I felt a small quiver between my legs. Basil spread my legs farther apart and then began to rub the top of my soft, velvety bush with his fingers. He moved them in slow, circular motions, and my box flexed and released with each revolution of his hand.

"Your pussy smells so good," he whispered. Then he placed his face between my legs and took another long inhale.

"Aaaggh," he breathed out. Then he put his mouth to me, sticking out his tongue and licking between my waiting lips and all around my swollen, wanting clitoris. Tasha was still sucking and nibbling on my breasts, and I reached up and unhooked her halter top. Her full, perky breasts fell on top of me, and I took them in my hands. With his face still between my legs, Basil unbuttoned Tasha's jeans and his own and pulled them off. He stuck his tongue deep inside of me and flicked it forcefully back and forth. My stomach caved, and I moved to meet his mouth. Then he took his finger and slid it up into my womb and back out again. He licked the warm cream off his middle finger and then stuck two of them back inside me and moved them in and out, and so I moved to meet his hand. He never moved his hand away while he stood up and kissed Tasha on the mouth. She wrapped her arms around him and slid down his waist to his already more than erect penis. Tasha was a lot of things but she was no liar. It was big. It was pretty. And it was perfect. And, when he stood, it reached way past his navel and seemed to throb and sway all by itself. It was so not Barry that I wanted to have it inside me immediately.

But Tasha had other plans for Basil's beautifully thick and

flawless manhood. She slid down his body and wrapped her arms around his legs, planting her face right between his legs. He held his tremendous dick in his hands and guided it slowly into her expectant mouth. He closed his eyes and let out a deep sigh. She gripped his smooth, tight butt in her hands and pulled him into her. He fell down on the bed next to me, and she climbed on top of his legs, never once removing his instrument from her mouth. He reached over and pulled me on top of his face. I didn't move at first, but he kept pulling me into him so I began to rock with the motion of his tongue inside me. At first, I felt a little awkward but, when I got the hang of him, I came on him, shivering and dripping my warm fluid down his cheeks and chin. Then Tasha rose and straddled his body. She sat down on his penis and wrapped her arms around me in one motion, and we all trembled. As she rocked, I rocked, and as I shook, she shook; the three of us all in one sublime, magnificent motion together.

In a moment there was a turning, and Tasha was laid on her back on the bed and Basil stood between her legs, pounding her flesh with his rock-hard shaft.

"Come to me," she said to me, and I did. "Sit on me," she said. And I straddled her face exactly as I had done Basil's. His heavy motion encouraged me to move even more and her warm, wet mouth sent shivers up my spine. I could feel him grabbing for my butt. Then he pulled out of Tasha and walked around the bed in front of me. He grabbed me by my shoulders and lifted me up off his girlfriend's face and turned me over onto all fours. Then, he spread my butt cheeks in his giant hands and rammed his perfect cock deep into my pulsating pussy. I moaned, and Tasha came and stood in front of me on the bed. She yanked my head up by my hair and smashed my face into her box. I opened my mouth and grabbed her full mound of hair lightly between my teeth. Then I licked her clit, moving quickly back and forth with my tongue. It was the first time I had ever been between another woman's legs. It was softer than I had imagined. It was hotter. And Tasha's pussy was incredibly wet, and she was dripping down her own legs and on my chin and cheeks and neck. I stuck my tongue out and scooped as much of her juice as I could out from the entrance to her womb. She was sizzling. She tasted salty and sweet and funky and ripe and hot, and I dug my face into her as far as I could go. Behind me, Basil was stroking me hard and slow, careful not to ram into me too hard. I pushed Tasha down on the bed and lay down between her legs with my butt tooted upward. That way Basil could hit it as hard as he wanted. I ate her beautiful, sweet-tasting pussy and her man screwed me from the back until I had no more feeling left between my legs. I came on his fat, solid dick over and over. And Tasha came for me over and over. I lapped up her sugary libations and finally, just as Basil pulled out of me and sprayed an ocean of hot syrup on my back and butt, I fell down on her chest, and we all collapsed in a pile together.

As I lay there between them, I thought about how bland my life had been. How boring and flavorless and "white" it was. And I was so happy to have a friend as crazy and wild and as bright fire-red as Tasha. I loved her for who she was. And although I was never meant to be as vibrant as she, I thought that maybe, from here on out, I just might be a little more on the pink side than usual.

And I also thought that maybe, just maybe, I would give good ol' Jameson with the pretty legs from the post office (and his girlfriend) a call.

Freeing Nikki

The day I married Curtis was the best day of my life. Everybody says that. Everyone says that the best day of their life was the day they married their husband or wife. Or the day their first child was born. But in the corners of their mind where they remember things they shouldn't be remembering, they quietly think that the best day was really the summer day they spent at Martha's Vineyard drinking Verde with their friends and watching women with big butts in small bathing suits. Sometimes they remember quietly that the best night of their life was spent with someone they hardly knew dancing together in a roomful of people as if no one was watching and then making love under the stars on the hood of their best friend's old Iroc Z-28. But for me, the day I married my husband was truly the best day of my life.

I loved Curtis in a way that I can hardly explain with my mouth. But my soul knew how. My soul knew him, and he knew my soul. Some days we talked and talked until the sun came up and only stopped because one of us finally had to get dressed for work. Some days we would sit quietly for hours, but it was as if we had been having the most intimate conversation. I loved him from the tip of his crooked toes to the top of his nappy head. I loved his smell. I loved his voice. I loved the way his eyes drooped in the morning. I loved the way he made love to me. And, though they tell me it's not healthy to love a man more than you love yourself, I know I loved him just that much.

I sat there on the bus that day remembering us. I remembered the way he used to rub my feet when I would come home tired and cranky. I remembered that I was always happy when he was around and when he was gone I was always searching for him; trying to find his smell on the bed, wrapping myself up in his clothes, cooking fettuccini Alfredo with shrimp because he would be happy to have a good meal when he came in the door. And then I remembered the first night he didn't make it home. And the first time he didn't call. And the first time I put my arm around his shoulders as we lay in the bed and he pulled away from me. And I knew, even then, that he would be leaving. I knew when his touch went cold that he had gone to someone else. And whenever I would ask him where he had been and what he had been doing he would look at me as if I was the one intruding and say: "I was doing what free Black men do." Like he had been a slave or something. And although he would never say it, I knew he had stopped loving me. And I sat there on the bus that day and cried.

"Sis" I heard a man's voice talking but it seemed at the time to be far in the distance. I was reliving my life; sitting there trying to keep my heart from exploding; certainly no one was talking to me.

"Sister," the voice said again. It was deep and gravelly. It was strong, and it shook me from my daze. "Here you go," the voice said, and a large brown hand reached out to me and handed me a tissue. "You're much too beautiful to be so sad."

Me? Beautiful? I looked up to tell this man that he must surely be mistaken. If I was beautiful my husband would be home when I got there. If I was beautiful he would want to touch me. He would say he loved me. He would call. He would, least of all, call. I was going to tell this man that he was as big a fool as I, but when I looked up, his eyes were looking at me as if he could see straight through my skin. And I could not speak at all.

He was a brown man, though lighter than I was. His skin was honey colored and his eyes were black like the jungle night. There was nothing false about them. They were strong eyes, accompanied by thick black eyebrows and full lips that were a little square in the corners the way a man's lips should be. He wore a mustache and goatee that were freshly trimmed and when his mouth moved I forgot I was sad.

"I would never make you cry like that," he said to me.

"You couldn't," I said. After all, you have to love someone to hate someone. You have to need someone to mourn his loss. I didn't know this man. He didn't know me. "You couldn't," I repeated.

"I wouldn't is the difference," he said and sat back in his chair, leaving his tissue on my knee and innocently touching my leg in the process. It was hot, and the air conditioner on the bus was only half working. But his hand felt good there. It felt good to be touched. Even if it was by accident. I dotted the tissue against my eyes and stopped crying.

"My name is Christopher," he said, extending his hand.

"Nicole," I said, taking his hand lightly. It was not the way I had been taught to shake, but I was not feeling assertive or strong. I was barely feeling anything, and it seemed my heart was feeling everything. Everything, but not strong.

"Let me take you out, Nicole." He leaned over and spoke to me softly. Even his whisper was powerful, and I was afraid. He was a gorgeous man. Nice enough. His shoulders were wide and solid, and I thought that he might just pick me up off this bus and walk me into Heaven.

"No," I told him. "I'm married."

"I see," he said.

The next day Christopher was on the bus again. Curtis had finally come home the night before. This time he was only gone for two days. I had already had a pedicure and a manicure done over the weekend. I took a shower and oiled my body with the vanilla essence that he used to say drove him bananas. I took my hair down from my customary ponytail and let it hang loosely on my shoulders. I put on my red satin nightgown with the splits that hit the ceiling. I lit scented candles while he was in the bathroom taking a shower. I put out a bowl of cherries and grapes and popped open a bottle of Chardonnay. He was my husband. And we were going to get this thing right. He was going to love me.

Curtis came out of the bathroom completely naked and shining from baby oil and cocoa butter. He was a fine man, slim built with chiseled muscles like a runner or a basketball player. He walked over to one of the candles and said, "What is this? Raspberry? It's making the room stink." And he blew it out and climbed into bed and turned his back to me.

I was reliving this when Christopher sat down next to me. "Hello, Ms. Nicole."

"Nikki," I said.

"Are you still married?"

I smiled one of those smiles. The kind we give when we are hurting but we are tired of crying. "I don't think so," I said, and he touched my leg as if we were friends. For a while we didn't talk and then, before his stop, he handed me his card: Christopher Young, Financial Analyst, with the address and home phone number handwritten on the back.

"Let me take you out?" he asked.

"No," I said. "I'm not ready to go out."

That night Curtis did not come home again and did not bother to call. I was so tired of trying. I don't think I had anymore tears left to give him. I didn't even feel him missing from the bed. I spread myself around, kicking my legs across his side and felt the coolness of the sheets on my naked calves. I rubbed my hands across the surface of the bed just to feel that same crispness and revel in the freedom of not missing him for the first time. My hand brushed against my leg, and I noticed it. I lifted my hand and rubbed it in circles on my thighs. Then I massaged my pelvis and guiltily moved my fingers between my legs. My body was new to this. The only time it had been touched in weeks was with a loofah in the shower. I shivered when my forefinger ran across my clitoris. Then I stopped. I did not want to do this. I did not want to be touching myself. I wanted someone else to touch me. To hold me. To make me shiver. On the third day when Christopher got on the bus, I smiled at him.

"Would you like to take me out, Mr. Young?" I asked him.

"Chris," he said. "Get off the bus with me."

We lived in North Philadelphia, or at least I did. But we got off the bus at the art museum. It was dusk, and we walked back along the bike trail between the museum and the river. It was beautiful there. The sun set on the myriad of flowers and trees, and the light evening breeze possessed them to dance for us. As we walked, he reached out and grabbed my hand and then held it in his own, finger intertwined with finger. I had not held hands since the senior prom. Curtis thought it was corny but it felt good. Then we climbed the old stairs to the gazebo and watched the sun go down over the water. It was so pretty I almost forgot it was polluted. We talked for a while about me. He asked me questions about my life, about my day, about my plans and my dreams. Curtis and I had long since stopped talking dreams. Then Chris kissed me softly and night fell around us. Before we knew it, it was nearly eleven o'clock, and the trail and the museum were empty except for us and the river and the moon.

And then he kissed me again. This time not so softly. He pressed his full, firm lips up against mine and held his hand to the back of my head. My mouth had been open, anticipating his, but he slid his tongue along my bottom lip anyway, lowering it away from the top and allowing him more space. He sucked on my bottom lip gently and then wrapped his tongue around my own. He licked across the roof of my mouth, and I swiped my tongue across the front of his teeth and sucked his lips. He was so hot. I could feel his body moving toward mine and the heat from his lips and his chest and his groin...I moved my mouth away from his and began to kiss his neck. He smelled like a burning fireplace and spiced apples and vanilla and sweat. His shirt was open at the collar, and I bit his shoulder and he moaned.

"Oooh."

Oh my god, I thought. And a quiver went from my neck down to my panties. He let his hands fall to my behind. And then he massaged my butt and legs while he kissed my neck and chin and lips.

"We can stop," he said. "We can stop if you want to."

I unbuttoned his shirt the rest of the way. "No," I whispered. "I don't want to."

"You are so beautiful," he said to me. And he said it again. And I looked into his coal-black eyes to see if he was lying, but he was not. I was beautiful. He lifted me by my butt up onto the gazebo walls and spread my legs with his own. I kissed his chiseled chest and sucked on his nipples until I felt a hardness pressed up against my thigh. I didn't know whether to unbutton his pants or pull up my dress but he lifted my dress up over my head before I had time to choose. Then he stood back and looked at me, but only long enough to smile. He took one of my full breasts into his massive hand. My nipples pointed to his mouth, and he obeyed their command. He opened his warm lips and wrapped then around my breast, and it seemed to melt and then come alive again in his mouth. With his other hand, he held me tightly up against him, and I could feel his heart beating in his penis. I wanted to see it. Surely it was beautiful. Surely it was as big and strong and beautiful as he. I unbuttoned his pants, and they fell to the gazebo floor. He was not wearing underwear, and his manhood stood on end, curving slightly to the right. The head was huge, and it glistened in the light from the stars, as did his sweaty chest, as did the spit he left on my breasts, as did my eyes when I finally saw his full naked glory. His shoulders were big and round and his hips and butt were tight and muscular, promising power. He held his penis in his hands and stroked it slowly. It was like he was calling me. Like he was teasing me, dangling a huge piece of paradise in front of my face. My mouth dropped open, and I climbed down off the wall and took him into my own hands.

I could feel the dampness between my legs grow to a mighty river. He slid his hand up between my thighs and rubbed my kitten's lips, and she began to purr.

"I want you so bad," he said. "I have wanted you for so long. I've just been waiting. Just waiting."

I didn't respond. But I did take his huge steel manhood into one hand and wipe it across the wet entrance of my waiting cunt. No, I couldn't put it in yet. He had been so sweet. I had to taste him. I had to see what this massive instrument felt like in my mouth. I had to know if he was sweet through and through. And I bent down and kissed the head of his dick. Then I licked it hard with my tongue and finally swept it up between my lips and into my mouth. It went straight to the back of my throat. I could smell the sweat from his loins, and I liked it. I moved my tongue around in small circles, sucking on the shaft as hard as I could. He braced himself on the wall for support. I wanted him inside me. I wanted him to stick his big dick way inside of me and fill me up. I was so empty. And with this tool he could fill me up and set me free. And I wanted him to come. I wanted to feel as good as he made me feel. But he wouldn't. He grabbed me by the back of my hair and yanked me away from him. The he lifted me by my shoulders and placed me back up on the wall. I was naked, and I could feel the warmth of the concrete under my butt. It was like another lover there to keep me from falling.

Chris kissed me in the mouth again hard and said, "No. Let me." And he dropped to his knees and buried his face between my legs. An ocean of pearl-colored juices sprang from my wells the moment his tongue touched my clit. It had been so long. I knew I was wrong but I didn't care. I thanked God for this moment anyway. He sucked on the lips and drove his tongue deep inside my womb, flicking it faster and faster and in circles and then in and out, out and in, until I came. And then came again. He took my clitoris between his lips and sucked and then nibbled it lightly with his front teeth. I pulled on his short, curly afro, and he didn't seem to mind. He just kept eating. Then he flattened his tongue and pressed it against me, licking me from the top of my mound all the way back to my butt. It tingled at his kiss and then he moved his tongue forward again. I wanted to scream but I held it in only because we were outside. Then he raised himself up, and, in one movement, stuck his huge shaft deep inside of me, and I did scream. Loud. Any witnesses be damned.

He filled me up in a way I have never been filled. His dick throbbed inside of me, and I could feel each heartbeat in my walls. I clenched my muscles together and held him tightly inside. He grabbed my hair, and I held on to his tight butt, pressing him forward, encouraging him in deeper with each thrust.

"Please," I said. "Please. Please. Please. Pleeaase." I cried, although I do not know exactly what I was begging for. More than anything, I think it was "Please give me all of this. Please don't stop screwing me. Please fill me up. Please don't let me go."

I came on him, and it was as if someone had opened a dam.

I flooded him with all of my juices. I gave him everything I had been longing to give away, but had no one with whom to share it. And when he felt me quiver and then drench his fat penis with all of my juices, he exploded inside of me, allowing me to share the warmth of his own current. My pussy tingled and pulsated again, quivering at the feeling of him busting open inside of me and then spilling out of the sides. I wrapped my legs around his and pulled him into my body. I held his neck and laid my head on his shoulder. He wrapped his huge arms around my back.

"It's okay, Nikki."

"Thank you," I said.

When I came in the door, Curtis was sitting at the dining room table looking dumbly at an empty placemat.

"How come you didn't cook?" he asked me. "Where you been? What you been doing?"

Doing what free Black men do," I told him and walked up the stairs to my bedroom and closed the door.

His bags were packed and on the stairs before he woke up the next morning. Curtis had given me both the best and the worst days of my life...until yesterday, I thought, dumping another trash bag full of his clothes down the stars. The day I married him had been my life's joy. That is, until the day I was freed. I looked at my watch, then, and hurried upstairs to the shower. Lord knows I did not want to miss my bus.

Spanish 101

Every teacher everywhere knows that there are two days you are most likely not to have anybody sitting in your classroom. That is rainy Mondays and sunny Fridays. Especially if, like me, you teach adults, who are notorious for non-attendance. Even for credited classes, in night school, whether it's GED or PhD, everything comes before class: "Oh, Miss Roberts, the water department had to do work in my basement, and I couldn't leave them in the house alone." "Oh, Professor Roberts, my twins have the chicken pox, and I couldn't leave them in the house alone." "Sorry, we had mandatory overtime last week. I couldn't get out of it." But that's the nature of grown folks. They have business.

So I was sitting in my classroom alone on this rainy Monday evening taking advantage of the solitude by grading some papers that I had never returned and which now seemed to be growing like weeds up out of my briefcase.

"You here by yourself, Miss Lady Ma'am?" the guard asked, peeking into the classroom.

"Looks like it, " I answered.

"Guess it's the rain," he said. "People think they're made of sugar."

"Come again?" I said.

"These folks think they'll melt if they get a little wet. If I was in your class, I'd be here every day. Hell, I'd be here on the days you wasn't here, just in case. I could learn a lot just sittin' outside the door of a smart lady like you."

I smiled. He was a cute guy, probably in his mid-twenties, just a few years younger than me. But he was from the Midwest somewhere, and he seemed country, and he talked loud and slow.

"Thanks," I said. "That's nice of you to say." I put my head back down into my stack of papers thinking he would move on down the hallway to converse with some other pretty professor sitting alone in her classroom, but he did not move. I could feel him still watching me from the door so I looked up.

"Yes?"

"What's your name, ma'am?"

"Roberts. Marie Roberts. What's yours?"

"Dwayne. Dwayne Cheshire, ma'am. What course is this here?"

"African-American Women Writers. It's an English course."

"Oh. That sounds nice, ma'am. A course on Black lady writers. That's nice."

"How old do I look to you, Dwayne?" I asked.

"I don't know. Round about my age. Round about twenty-five or thirty," he guessed, almost correctly. I would be thirty-three in a couple of weeks. But it was damn good to hear I could still pass for twenty-five.

"And how old are you?" I asked.

"Twenty-seven, ma'am."

"Dwayne," I told him, "if my mother ever comes in this building, you can call her ma'am. If my grandmother ever comes here, you can certainly call her ma'am. But please call me Marie because you're make me feel a lot older than twenty-five or thirty."

"Yes, ma'am."

"Dwayne!"

"Marie."

"That's better. Now, I'm gonna mark the rest of these papers so I guess I'll see you around," I told him, fully expecting that he would catch the hint.

"Miss Marie?" He looked at me, smiling. Not exactly what I had in mind but Miss Marie was better than ma'am any day.

"Yeah?"

"You 'bout the prettiest night school college teacher I ever seen."

I laughed and flagged him away. "Thanks, Dwayne. See you later."

I marked about three or four more sorry attempts at analyzing the symbolism in *The Bluest Eye,* and I dropped my pen down on the table. This sucked. The rain sucked. Being here sucked. Being here alone really sucked. And if I was so pretty, how come I was still single and hadn't had sex in more than a year? That sucked most of all. It's funny the way your mind can move from a Pulitzer Prize-winning book to a bout with self-pity in such a small fragment of time. I packed all the papers back into my bag and started to head for home when the door opened and a sopping wet Daisy Trinidad entered the room.

"I am so sorry, Professor Roberts. I got here as soon as I could," she was saying, taking her soaked cotton jacket off and hanging it over a chair. Then she looked around the empty room. "Where is everybody?"

"I don't know. I thought you all had a party and didn't invite me," I told her. "I was just about to leave."

"Oh, man!" she said, pouting as she plopped herself down in one of the chairs. "Don't say that. You don't know how hard it was for me to get here."

I liked Daisy probably the best out of all my students. If anyone were going to show up for class, it would have been her.

She was smart and dedicated. She was about thirty as well, short and pretty and tan with long, thick, curly hair that was almost jet-black. She was busty but she tried to hide herself under baggy clothes and coveralls. I had a classroom full of twenty-year-old hoochies who came to class in the spring with their butts on the outside of their shorts and who were stupid enough to pay two hundred dollars a credit hour for a class and then not show up. Daisy was a refreshing change. I sat back down on the desk in front of her.

She had her head in her hands, wet hair clinging to her face and shoulders.

"What's wrong, Daisy?" I asked. She looked upset and, although she was not crying I could tell she was only minutes from breaking down.

"It's just problems, Professor. It's just relationship problems."

"Oh," I said, prepared to back off. I tried not to get into things like that. People were funny. They figured if you could teach them to read, you could teach them how to fix all their problems, and I was relationship disabled myself.

"I just wanted to come to class so bad. And my boyfriend always drives me. But we got in a big fight in the car, and he put me out halfway, and no buses were running so I had to walk all the way here."

"Are you serious?" I said. "In all this rain?" I paused for a moment. Now even I wouldn't have been that dedicated. "Well you are a really dedicated student. I guess I better stay and teach you something, huh?"

Daisy smiled and for the next hour we had a surprisingly intellectual conversation about the rest of Toni Morrison's works. At nine o'clock the lights in the hallway flashed indicating that we had fifteen minutes to leave the building or we would be locked in.

"Can I give you a ride, Daisy?" I asked her.

"Thank you," she said to me.

In the car on the way to her house we stopped being teacher and student and just talked. She told me about her boyfriend and how terrible his temper was. I told her about my old love life (since I didn't have a new one) and how I had once had to leave a man with a temper that sounded very much like her boyfriend's.

As she backed out of the car, she said, "I'm really glad I came today. You're the only reason I come anyway. Thanks for the ride." And she closed the car door and ran up her steps. I didn't know what she meant by that but I figured that if Daisy had not been my student, she probably would have been my friend.

After the next class, during which I spent fifteen minutes lecturing the students about their responsibility to their own education and the stupidity of paying for something and then not using it, I had five students waiting to speak to me one-on-one. Every conversation was the same. "I had to do this." "I'm sorry but my kids that." And I cut their excuses down one by one until the only person left standing in my room was Daisy Trinidad.

"Marie," she called me. She had never called me Marie, even though I had told her to on many occasions. "I just wanted to thank you for the ride the other day. Oscar and I broke up. It's over."

"How do you feel?" I asked.

"I don't know. He was just so jealous, and I couldn't control him, and he couldn't control himself."

"Jealous?"

"Yeah."

"Of what? Of other men? Of you getting your education?" I had seen that before. It happened a lot that when one partner went back to school to better him or herself, the other partner tried to bring them down out of jealousy or insecurity.

"No. He was jealous of you."

I sat down in my chair and looked at her. Me? "Me? Why

me?"

"Well I would always come home and tell him how smart and pretty you are and how you really have it goin' on and everything. And he would listen. But then one day I told him that you had on a really sexy skirt and boots, and he said that I sounded like a man the way I talked about you. Like I wanted to, well you know."

I was stunned. I couldn't talk for a minute. What exactly was she saying? Did she admire me like a role model? Did she like my fashion savvy? Was she trying to hit on me? What the hell was this conversation about?

"Well," I answered diplomatically, "I'm sorry about your breakup, and if I had anything to do with it, I apologize."

"No," she said, sitting down in the chair in front of me. "It's not you. It's me. I just really like you is all."

I didn't say anything. What is like? What does that mean?

"I just really like you," she repeated and walked out of the room.

That night Daisy was stuck to my mind like Krazy Glue. I couldn't figure out the deal. And as for me, I liked boys. But it wasn't like I didn't know a sexy woman when I saw one. And Daisy definitely fit the bill. And it wasn't like I hadn't had a semi-experience with a woman before but that was back in cheerleading camp, and we were just practicing our kissing styles on each other before we used them on anybody else. I could hardly think straight so I went straight to bed. In my dreams, a woman, not Daisy, cornered me in a closet and lifted me up on her shoulders and proceeded to give me head. She was obviously a very strong woman and I came in my sleep several times and awoke to find myself humping on a pillow. So, I had never thought about...about...I couldn't even say it really. And the worst part was, she may have meant something totally different and I was here going crazy and humping bedding.

During the next class, Daisy was pretty quiet. She didn't raise

her hand or volunteer any insight. She sat in the back and lis-
tened, and when class was over she headed for the door just like
everyone else.

"Miss Trinidad," I called to her, "can I see you for a moment?"

When the room had emptied, I closed the door and sat down
on the desk. I had been losing my mind all weekend. And I
knew why. If it had been another student, or any male student,
I would probably have reprimanded them, told them that their
behavior was inappropriate given the context of our relationship
and that I didn't expect to have to talk about it again. But I
liked Daisy. Somewhere, where I wasn't supposed to be thinking of her, I was thinking of her. I wasn't supposed to be noticing her hair or her eyes or her chest or her clothes and yet I
could recall every outfit she had worn since the first day of class.
I had to know what she meant. I would deal with it later but I
had to find out exactly what it was I was dealing with.

"Yes?" She looked up at me. "Is something wrong with my
paper?"

"No," I told her. "Your work is fine. You're doing beautifully. It's just..." I paused. Too late. Had to say something now.
"What exactly did you mean when you said that you liked me?"
Oh, that sounded perverted even coming out. "I mean, if it's
my teaching style and so forth, what exactly is it that you like so
I can make sure to do it in all my classes?" I tried to clean it up
but it was too late. She laughed a little and stood and took a
step toward the door. Then she took a step toward me.

"I like you," she said. "*Te gusto.* I think you are smart and
pretty and sophisticated." She took another step toward me. "I
think you are beautiful and funny and sexy." She took another
step and then took my face in her hands. I didn't pull away. It
felt nice. "I think you are *muy caliente y yo deseo besarmo sus....*"
She stopped. And it was a good thing because my Spanish was
rusty. But she bent down and kissed me smack on the lips. "*Sus
labios,*" she finished. "*Y sus hombres,*" she said, and she kissed me

on the place between my neck and my shoulders. "*Y los pechos,*" she said, and she traced my breasts with her finger. I was supposed to be telling her how wrong this was and how much trouble we could both get into. But her lips felt so good on my neck that I forgot what I was supposed to be saying, and I just went with what I was feeling. "*Profesora Marie, usted desea tocarme?*" I knew that much. Did I want to touch her? *Si.* Yes. I most definitely did.

I touched my hand gently to her face and pressed my lips against hers. They were soft, softer than I remembered lips to be. And she opened her mouth and slid her tongue between my teeth, licking the roof of my mouth and sucking my lips at the same time. I wrapped my arms around her waist and pulled her closer to me. I was still sitting on the desk, and she stood between my legs. She started kissing me on the neck and licking my ears, whispering things in Spanish that sounded like sex even if I didn't know what they meant. "*Tocarme, profesora. Soy tan mojado. Soy tan mojado.*"

I pulled her baggy Polo shirt up over her head revealing her beautiful almond-colored breasts. They were fuller than I had imagined, and they were pressed together in her purple satin bra, which I quickly removed. I ran my fingers over them slowly. Her nipples were light colored and large, and I traced one with my finger before putting it to my mouth. She smelled sweet, like pears; soft, the way women should smell. I sucked on her velvety breasts, licking her around her nipples and nibbling on them lightly. She bent over me and unzipped the back of my dress. Then she traced my own caramel-colored breasts with her fingers and undid my bra. She kissed me again on the mouth and then kissed her way down my chin and neck to my chest. My nipples were as hard as glass, and she fingered them lightly, smiling before she wrapped her mouth around them. I leaned back on the desk to give her more room to work with. A light flashed somewhere in the hallway. I undid my bun, and my tousled hair fell to my shoulders. Then I closed my eyes.

In a few moments she was sliding my dress down over my hips and pulling my panties down with it. I tried hard not to think of what was happening. How I could let myself be seduced so easily? I thought only of how good she felt. How sweet she smelled. How warm her body was.

When she had stripped me totally, I lay on the table naked and anxious but I did not move. I felt her lips on my ankle. She kissed me there tenderly and then again on my calf.

"*Deseo probarle*." she said. "*Deseo probar su gatito.*"

She kissed my legs all the way up to where my inner thighs met in the middle. Then she stopped. I let out a soft breath, and she smiled again. "Not yet," she said in English. "We save the best for last."

She climbed on top of me, straddling my body with her legs, pushing her soft mound up against my own. It is a thing I always wondered about: how grinding up against another woman's pussy could turn someone on. But it did, and I felt a tingling down between my legs I hadn't felt in months. (Fourteen months, two weeks, two days to be exact.) She sat on top of me swirling her rounded hips up in small rings. I could feel the dampness from her own warm pussy begin to seep out onto mine. She bent over and pressed her breasts up against mine and took one into her mouth. Then, as she started to kiss me on the lips again, I felt her hand between my legs. At first she just massaged down there, kneading the top where the hair was shaved, and then moving the lips together and apart again slowly. When she stuck her tongue in my mouth, she also stuck her middle finger up inside me, and my body quivered. "Oh," I said.

"I know, *Mommi*," she said. "This is what I've been trying to tell you."

She added another finger and moved them in and out of me slowly until I felt myself pushing her hand into me harder and faster. She smiled at me, and I wondered how soft and warm her own little cat would feel.

I scooted down on the desk and as she raised her hips up off me, I pushed her up toward my face. I could feel her heat when she was still a foot away. She was waiting for me, and before I could even put my mouth to her she was dripping on my chin. I licked it away and sat her down on my face. She didn't move, at first. And, at first, I just played with her clit with my tongue, flicking it back and forth and sucking it lightly now and again. When she began to breathe a little harder, I dug my chin into the entrance of her steaming body, just to let her know I was there. She moaned, and I sucked on her lips, first one and then the other. I could feel her walls throbbing; coming apart and then clinging together again.

"Stick your tongue in me, Profesora," she begged. "Stick your tongue inside me. Please."

I laughed and obliged. I stuck my tongue as far inside her womb as it would go. A river of hot, salty juices poured out of her body and onto my chin. I rammed my face into her a few good times, and she began to move her hips back and forth. I grabbed her butt and pushed her closer since that was where she wanted to be. I ate her pussy until she couldn't talk in Spanish or English. Then I took my tongue away and sucked on her shining labia one more time. She came again, and I scooted her down slowly away from my face.

On the way down she regained her composure and dove straight for me tongue first. She flattened her tongue and licked me from the rear of my pussy all the way up to my clit three times before she said, "Turn over." I obliged her again.

I sat on top of the desk on all fours, my butt sticking into the air. She rammed her finger into my hole again, this time harder than before. I moaned, and she did it again. Then she moved her hand around slowly as she bent down to suck my clit at the same time. Cream-colored jism dripped down her hand.

"You like me, too, huh?" she asked.

"*Si. Te gusto. Te gusto mucho,*" I answered, and she removed her fingers and replaced them with her long, fat tongue. I fell flat to the table, and she spread my legs out wide, pulling my hips back toward her face and ramming her tongue into my crotch. I came again. And again. And one more time after that. When she was full, she climbed up and lay on top of me, her firm box rubbing against my soft behind. She fingered my hair and kissed the back of my neck.

"So can I get an A?" she asked.

"You already had an A," I told her.

"Not in the English class" she said. "In the Spanish class."

"An A-plus," I answered.

We dressed and walked into the hallway, which was now dark. Dwayne, the guard, was sitting outside the door.

"Dwayne! What are you still doing here?" I asked him.

"I heard noises, ma'am. I came to check 'em out."

"And what did you find?" I asked him.

"Nothing," he said.

"That's more than nothing," Daisy said, pointing to his pants, his rock-hard dick trying to poke a hole through his security-guard polyesters.

"We're locked in," Dwayne said. "The warning light flashed an hour ago."

"Oh, well," Daisy said, smiling. "I guess we can go back and finish our lesson until someone comes to open the door."

"I guess we can," I said. And we turned to go back in the classroom. "But what are you going to do, Dwayne?"

"I'll just stay out here and wait, if you two don't mind, ma'am," Dwayne said. "Like I told ya, I can learn a whole lot just sitting outside your door."

Daisy and I smiled and closed the door again.

Impulse

by
Montana Blue

Chapter One

Traffic on the Woodson Expressway was mercifully light for a Monday morning. Cassandra Hearst put her white Supra into third gear and mused over her appointments. As CEO of DirectData, the largest credit-card processor in the Midwest, she loved everything about her job, except what she had to do today—listen to presentations from vendors trying to sell her something.

The downtown Minneapolis skyline came into view. Cassandra inched the speedometer to seventy-five and cranked up the air conditioner. Only seven a.m. and already the outdoor temperature gauge on her dash read eighty-nine degrees. Another scorcher, she thought. So far, this had been the hottest summer she could remember since relocating from Tucson. At least there, the heat was dry and more tolerable. But in Minneapolis the heat came with a humidity that made everything sweat like pigs at a barbecue. Sometimes it was beyond unbearable. Cassandra gazed out toward the cityscape in the horizon. Some mornings as she drove in, it seemed as though the buildings were moving toward her instead of the other way around. And each year it took less and less time for her to reach the fringes of the city because of all of the expansion westward. In the last six months, she had seen two high-rise, apartment complexes built and the groundbreaking of a third. She looked to her left and read the sign as she approached the new development. Brookhaven Townehomes. They look expensive, she thought, taking the east curve of the expressway like a pro.

Suddenly, she heard an explosion that echoed like a gunshot in her ears, and her car skidded out of control. Frantically, she pumped the brake and fought the steering wheel as the Supra went careening off the road. After a few horrific seconds, Cassandra brought the vehicle to a halt.

Heart beating wildly and hands shaking, she lowered her head to the steering wheel. She took several deep breaths to calm herself then stepped out of the car to assess the damage. The thick heat sucked her breath away and drew her clothes to her as if her skin were magnetized.

Her right front tire looked like a mound of black clay draped over a silver Frisbee.

"The heat will do strange things," a deep voice said from behind her.

Cassandra spun around and looked up. Towering over her was a man whom her senses told her could probably make her do strange things. She was uncharacteristically speechless.

"Do you have a spare?"

"Yes," she said, and pressed a button on her key chain. The trunk sprang open. She walked to the back of the car, heels clicking against the asphalt. She had been so mesmerized by the handsome stranger that she forgot about her roadside assistance club.

"I'm sorry, uh..." She gestured toward him.

"August," he said, lifting the mat in her trunk with one hand and hoisting the spare tire out with the other. Cassandra watched the biceps on his arms bulge into granite like rocks.

"August, I have roadside assistance and a cell phone. But thanks for the offer." As the words trailed from her lips, she moaned internally while he propped the tire against the car and went back to the trunk for the jack. She could see tiny pearls of sweat glistening against his body. He looked lickable.

"By the time the truck gets here, I'll already have you serviced," he said, and tilted his head to the side.

Service me, she thought.

"You need any help, man?" someone from the building site called.

"No," August replied, looking backward. Then he returned his gaze to Cassandra. "I got this."

She watched intently as he went once more to her trunk. He walked with a rhythm in sync with the sounds of metal striking metal, pile drivers, and loud orders being given around them. After a few moments, his words disturbed the air between them. "You don't seem to have a wrench."

Cassandra's hand touched her neck lightly as she watched his mouth. He had the kind of lips that just begged to be kissed. Very round and very sensual. They were moving but she felt as though all sound had been drawn from their midst. And she was caught in a vacuum. And oh God . . . now he was licking them.

"I'm sorry, what?" she said, slightly unnerved and flushed.

"I'll be right back," he said, and walked toward the construction zone.

What am I doing? Cassandra asked herself, pacing. And then her line of sight caught and held on the blue jeans August was wearing. He must have been poured into them. The view of his backside was mouth watering, and she gave it a thorough appraising.

Starting from the narrow waist then traveling down to a pair of glutes so symmetrical and tight you could bounce a quarter off them. Then on to massively muscular thighs. Then...

Stop it, she reprimanded herself. A few moments longer and she would have been drooling. She decided to do the practical thing and call the office. She walked back to the driver's side of the vehicle and retrieved a cell phone from her purse. Quickly, she dialed the numbers. Lawrence Hayes, her administrative assistant, answered on the first ring.

"Cassandra Hearst's office. Larry speaking. May I help you?"

"Good morning, Larry."

"Ms. Hearst? Is anything wrong?"

Nothing a fine specimen of Black man can't fix. "Flat tire."

"Shall I cancel your morning appointment?"

"Push it back if you can. I want to get this over with today."

Like testosterone radar, Cassandra picked up August on her man-meter before she even saw him. Her senses had gone into overdrive. He returned, power drill in hand.

She fanned herself at his approach, certain she could pass off the gesture as a response to the heat. And by her standards the temperature was increasing with each sensuous movement of August's body.

"Ms. Hearst?"

"That will be all, Larry. I'll be in soon."

Flipping her cell phone closed and returning it to her purse, all she could think about was the hands that were holding the drill. How masterful they looked. She imagined the roughness she saw in them moving stealthily across her thighs, igniting her skin like a tinderbox. Suddenly her body felt ablaze with need. She walked toward him like steel to a magnet.

The spinning sound of bolts twisting free of the spokes resonated on her body. The traffic whooshing by vibrated her insides. Her entire being leaped to life. And the temperature was getting hotter by the minute. Again, she fanned herself.

August looked up with the movement of her hand. He gave her a slow, brazen examination from head to toe and then back to head.

"It's hot already. And," he added, sliding a moist tongue across his lips, "so early."

"Yes, it is," she responded, attraction lowering her voice an octave.

"This won't take long, Miss. Miss?"

"Cassandra."

"Cassandra," he repeated.

Coming from his mouth, her name sounded like the ocean— wide and inviting. He returned to his work, and Cassandra was resigned to watch him. More and more, his body glistened wet with sweat. After a few moments, she could see where the moisture from his chest and arms made dark rings spread across his white, sleeveless T-shirt. The sight of it beckoned to her and aroused her beyond all sensibility.

"Almost there," he said. Standing, he placed his hand on the jack handle and pumped it up and down to lower the car. The movement sent her pulse racing and made her think impure thoughts, carnal thoughts, that could easily get her into trouble. While she stood speechless, August collapsed the jack and placed it, along with her ragged tire, back into the trunk. He wiped his hands on his jeans with a sliding motion that made it easy for her to see his solid thigh muscles. Then he took a quick swipe across his brow and removed the sweat that had formed there. She was enjoying this entirely too much. It was time to go.

"Thank you so much, August. I can't tell you how grateful I am for your help. And you were right. I would still be waiting for the motor club to come and rescue me if it hadn't been for you."

"It was my pleasure," he said, closing the trunk.

His words wrapped around Cassandra's libido with more than one meaning.

"I feel as if I owe you," she said, inspecting his work. The doughnut-sized tire would hold her until she could get to an auto repair shop and purchase a full-size one.

"Don't," he said, stepping closer. "I was glad to do it."

He was so close, she could smell his scent. Not foul or tart, just all man. It awoke something in her that had lain dormant for longer than she cared to think about. Before she did something foolish or embarrassing, she summoned the last vestiges of her composure.

"Well, I'd better go. I'm late as it is."

August said nothing. Just continued to look at her with eyes that ravaged her body. She imagined that they must be a sight standing so close. She with her French-rolled hair and her business-blue suit—complete with miniskirt and matching pumps. And he in his construction clothes, that were definitely putting in overtime. What a contrast they must have made.

She turned to leave and headed for the car. It was fixed and ready to go. She could feel his eyes upon her as surely as if he had been touching her with his hands. She opened the driver's side door and heard her name once more upon his lips.

"Cassandra," he said.

And she understood. It wasn't a call, or anything she needed to respond to. Just the last connection between them before the tie was severed forever. She closed the door behind her, determined not to look back. What she wanted to do with that man was a shame she thought as goose bumps prickled her skin. It had nothing to do with his helpfulness. It had even less to do with his good looks. It had nothing to do with anything except raw, animal magnetism. Since the moment she'd seen him, all she'd wanted to do was straddle him and hump herself into oblivion.

She started the car and sped away, determined to put the prurient thoughts of August out of her mind. *How about some oldies?* she asked herself turning on the radio.

"Do me, baby," The Artist now known again as Prince sang.

"Dang," she replied, changing to another station on the programmed dial.

"Szzzzz, rope burn," Janet sang at her sultry best.

"Damn," Cassandra protested, changing channels again.

The strong male vocal of R. Kelly was no better. *"Sex me, sex me, baby."*

This can't be happening, she thought, switching the dial once more to her favorite pop station. Madonna's "Deeper and Deeper" flowed tauntingly out of the speakers. Frustrated, Cassandra turned the radio off. She gripped the steering wheel tighter and straightened in her seat. *I am CEO of a Fortune 1000 company,* she reminded herself. But at that moment she felt about has strong as the washing end of a wet mop.

"August," she said, nearing downtown Minneapolis, "the month and man are definitely hot."

Chapter Two

At first, Cassandra had been grateful that Larry was able to push back her appointment. The vendor had agreed to come two hours later. But now, in the middle of the PowerPoint presentation, Cassandra found her mind wandering as it had all morning. Actually fixated was more like it. The more she thought about August and his tight pants and bulging muscles, the more aroused she became. And now, after mulling him over again and again in her mind, she had worked herself into a state that could only be cured by one thing—molten hot sex.

Cassandra fidgeted with the handouts on the table in front of her. She shifted positions in her chair several times. She crossed and uncrossed her legs. But, to no avail. The throbbing at the apex of her thighs would not be abated. It took all of her willpower not to hold herself like men sometimes do until she could cool down.

And it didn't help that a group of men was making this sales presentation. One by one, Cassandra had mentally disrobed them all, only to be disappointed. None of them measured up to what she had imagined in August earlier that morning.

"Ms. Hearst?"

"What?" she snapped, perturbed that she was shaken loose from her fantasies. She had just gotten to the part where August was licking the inside of her upper thigh.

Linc Verelli, her VP of marketing, leaned into her ear. "Is something wrong, Cassandra?"

"No," she lied. "Let's take a break," she suggested. She checked the wall thermostat on her way out of the conference room. It read a cool sixty-eight degrees. Darn her libido! She couldn't blame her elevated temperature on poor air conditioning.

She went to her office and entered her private bathroom. It was decorated in the tropical colors of dusty coral, turquoise, and deep orange. There were exotic seashells placed on the sink, towel table, and cabinet shelf. She stood in front of the mirror and didn't recognize the face she saw.

When she'd left home that morning, she'd been the wheeling and dealing Cassandra she'd always been—the Cassandra who was often stopped by strangers and asked where she was from. Some even ventured a guess. "Are you from Nigeria?" they would ask. One poor woman asked, "Are you African?" To which Cassandra responded, "Now what do you think?"

But Arizona-born Cassandra Hearst, was as American as jazz. However her features were distinctly African and substantially regal.

A prominent forehead, feline eyes, lofty cheekbones, angular nose, and luxurious mouth along with her five-foot-eleven-inch frame had allowed her to pursue modeling as a hobby during her twenties.

Even without makeup her features were striking. But she prided herself mostly on her poker face. In a business as cutthroat as banking and finance, it was important not to give away your hand until you were ready. But the face in the mirror told all. It reflected the needs and urges of a woman who hadn't been with a man in a long time. And she felt, and looked, vulnerable and exposed.

Where's the lioness that had slashed through her competition as if they were weak gazelles and clawed her way to the executive suite? It wasn't as if she hadn't seen handsome men before. Hell, some of the most handsome men she'd ever seen in life worked for her.

This August wasn't even what she would call drop-dead gorgeous. But something in the way his body disturbed the energy around her created a chemical reaction in her resembling cold fusion. She felt as though her body had been fashioned for the express purpose of pleasing and being pleased by him.

"Ms. Hearst?" came her secretary's familiar voice.

Cassandra turned and drew a quick, audible intake of breath.

"I'm sorry, didn't mean to startle you, ma'am, but they're waiting for you."

Aside from the occasional face job or salad toss from Larry, Cassandra hadn't fully experienced a man in more than four years. It seemed that every time she gave someone her entire body, her mind and soul went with it. So rather than lose herself again, Larry kept her lust at bay by being there whenever she needed him. Like bringing her a cup of coffee or interoffice mail, he would bring her to climax just as efficiently. And all that he asked in return was to be able to do it again whenever the occasion arose.

"Larry," she said, her voice barely above a whisper, "I need you." The randy expression on his face told her he recognized the call. He closed her office door and then approached.

She turned toward him as he entered the bathroom. Taking her well-practiced stance, she braced herself against the sink and spread her legs. Cassandra knew that he had somehow sensed her deep need. And to increase its urgency, he knelt before her with agonizing slowness. She reached out to him, and he moved away.

"No," he insisted. "No touching."

"Then hurry, please," she pleaded, trying to control her growing desire.

Larry kissed her ankles. "All in due time."

This man is a tease, she thought letting the sensation of his lips rising up her legs release her tension. His deliberate ascent made her shiver with anticipation as inch by inch he paid tribute to her skin with his lips and tongue. The higher his attentions, the wider Cassandra spread her legs. When he removed her panties, she trembled knowing full well what was to come next.

There was a pattern to Larry's ritual of consuming her. First, he would inhale her woman-scent with his nose gently bumping her clit. This soft teasing always made her feel liquid and golden. Then his hands would travel up her torso and massage her breasts through the fabric of her suit. This went on for several minutes until her succulent pink was drenched with wetness.

After that came the marvelous invasion of his tongue into her moist opening. And she would stand, trance like while he worked her into a frothy peak. By the time the third and forth orgasms gripped her, her fist would be in her mouth holding back the screams that threatened to give away their secret activity.

"You got it bad, Ms. Hearst. I can tell," he said, pausing for a moment. Tell-tale signs of her excitement glistened on his face. He licked the insides of her thighs where some of her precious juices had gotten away from him. "Why didn't you call me sooner? You know you never have to suffer. Not with me around."

He fingered her expertly with one hand and twirled a rock-hard nipple with the other. "You seem insatiable this morning. I can clear your schedule for the rest of the afternoon, Ms. Hearst. Maybe this time you'll let me feast on you the way I've always dreamed of."

Just then another climactic explosion overtook her. It left her panting and trembling for more. "Yes," he whispered. "Just like that…all afternoon."

"No, Larry. I…"

"I have a surprise for you," he interrupted. He stopped his pleasuring momentarily and reached inside his pocket. Cassandra recognized the object in his hand as a Tongue Teaser. She had seen them once in an adult emporium when she'd been shopping for a new vibrator. Deftly, Larry pulled the elastic end onto his tongue like a condom, which left the round, rubber end dangling off the tip. It was red and resembled a large cherry with ridges. He wagged his tongue like the thirsty animal he was and presumed to roll the teaser over her clit and into her slit. The feeling was new and exciting and made

Cassandra forget all about her meeting.

She almost gave their lustful game away when Larry placed the teaser directly on her clit and started a deep, reverberating hum. The sound vibrated the small, plastic bulb against her real one, and she cried out in ecstasy.

She grabbed the back of his head. "Do you want a promotion?" she rasped, stifling another scream.

"No," he replied.

"What then?" she asked, in the throes of yet another wild orgasm. When the contractions inside her subsided, Larry removed the Tongue Teaser.

"I want you. Wet and in my mouth. That's all."

Cassandra slumped over him. Sweat trickled down her neck and into the crevice between her breasts. He rose to his feet, picking her up with him—another regular part of the ritual. He sat her in her leather chair, and opened her bottom desk drawer. In it, he took out a box of wet naps and proceeded to clean away any traces of their interlude. He retrieved her panties from the bathroom and slid them up her legs, careful not to snag them on her garter.

Finally, he took a wet nap for himself and wiped his face thoroughly. "I could devour you 24/7."

This was his usual concluding response. Before he left, he turned and added, "You tasted exceptionally good today. Have you been with someone?"

Cassandra thought about August and wished that were the case. And although she had just had probably the best head of her life, what she really wanted was August. And the still pulsating crevice between her legs told her there would be no peace until she did.

Cassandra was defeated. For the first time in years, she felt completely helpless. Nothing she did would shake the hold August had on her. She had to regroup. And she couldn't do it at the office.

"Larry, I was incorrect earlier when I asked you to push back my appointment."

She stood up from her chair and ran a smoothing hand down her linen suit. "I'm going home. Please make my apologies to my staff and the members of Van Housen & Associates."

She removed her day planner from its stand on her desk. "See if you can reschedule the meeting for later this week. Check my schedule online. I should be available Thursday or Friday."

She reached the door to her office and turned to Larry now seated in his cubicle. "Oh, and Larry...cancel my two o'clock with Sheena from marketing and my three-thirty project update as well." "Yes, ma'am," Larry said as Cassandra whisked herself quickly out of her office and headed for home.

Usually, the soft glow of scented candles illuminated the bathroom. The water in the Jacuzzi would be hot and steaming, and the sounds of Maxwell or Will Downing would float crooning in from cordless speakers. Not today. Today the halogen lights blazed, the shower sprayed cool blasts of water, and her speakers proclaimed that Chaka Khan was every woman.

Even the soap she used to cleanse her body was different. It was Morning Sun, an aromatherapeutic blend of florals created to vitalize rather than relax. Invigorating. That's what the label said. But infuriating made a better descriptor. However, it was herself that caused the emotion not the bath gel. You'd think she'd never seen a man before. Or never been with one.

Cassandra grabbed a peach-colored towel from the rack and patted herself dry. The truth was that she hadn't, at least not like August. His allure was strong and almost sticky.

He's a construction worker, she admonished while pulling a fine-toothed comb through her wet hair—a hard hat for glory's sake! But it didn't matter. That man, with his rough hands and perspiration-soaked shirt, made her feel that what they say about a woman's sex drive in her thirties must be true.

She couldn't believe it. Two minutes out of the shower and if she wasn't careful, a fresh collection of her feminine juices would prompt her to take another. Putting on a silk tank and matching shorts, Cassandra realized that she hadn't gone fifteen minutes that day without thinking about some aspect of August.

Determined to loose herself from his lingering memory, she opened her mail. She channel-hopped from C-SPAN to CNBC to MSNBC. She logged on to the Internet where she checked her stock portfolio and made a few day trades. After that, she flipped through the *Wall Street Journal.* She had decided to fix herself a snack when the phone rang.

"Hello?"

"Hey, it's me."

"Hi, Jairus." She smiled. She should have known he would call. Jairus Flemming was VP of Financial Management for DirectData. Not only was he a genius with numbers, but he knew her like the back of his own hand.

The one that got away, she thought. Out of all her past relationships, their breakup was the only one she sometimes regretted. Her great consolation was the extraordinary friendship that resulted. He had an almost telepathic insight into her moods.

"How's Carol?" she asked.

"Fine."

"And the kids?"

"Ornery. But if they weren't, they wouldn't be mine. But that's not why I called, and you know it."

"Really?" she hedged.

"Really. You've never left in the middle of a meeting like that. And the brother making the presentation was on point. So, what's wrong?"

It was the third time that day someone had asked her that question. Cassandra sat down on her black leather sofa and sighed. "I met a man today."

"Oh."

She could hear the disappointment in Jairus' tone.

"Listen to you, Mr. Married with Children."

"I know. It doesn't stop me from being jealous, though."

Cassandra smiled.

"So…tell me about him."

"No."

"Why not?"

"Because I've just spent the last two hours trying to get him out of my head."

"Why would you do a thing like that?"

"Because ever since my blowout this morning, I haven't been able to fully concentrate on anything else."

"You had a blowout!"

Cassandra filled him in on all the details.

"And now he's mackin' your mind like Superfly."

"That's about the size of it."

"Damn, woman. You sound sprung."

Her skin warmed at the thought. "I can't even describe how sprung I feel."

For a few seconds, there was silence on the other end of the phone. And then Jairus cleared his throat. "More than when you were with me?"

Instantly the face and body of the man who had been her lover off and on for ten years appeared in her mind. He was a large man. Nearly seven feet tall and thick everywhere. And complementing that, was the face of an angel.

"Maybe."

"Well, I guess it had to happen sooner or later. So, when do you see him again?"

Cassandra's mind hadn't wrapped itself around that concept. "I don't! I can't."

"Why the hell not?"

"Because," she admitted, "I didn't get his phone number and he didn't ask for mine. Besides. I'm talking purely carnal, here. What I want with him doesn't require that we chitchat or make nice."

Jairus chuckled. "Then I guess you just better hope you don't have another blowout tomorrow."

Oh lord, tomorrow. That thought hadn't crossed her mind either. She might see him on the way in to work. She had intentionally taken a different route to return home. But during morning rush hour, she had to take the expressway unless she wanted to leave two hours early and drive through town.

She could just imagine driving past the site and conveniently standing near the curbside would be August in all his woman-wetting glory. She fantasized about her car slowing to the right and pulling up next to him. They needn't speak. Each of them would know what they wanted from the other. He would get in the car, and there, in front of God and Brookhaven's newest addition, they would..."

"Cassandra!"

She blinked away her fantasy and pulled the phone back up to her ear. "I'm sorry. I stepped out for a moment."

"I'll say. Hmmm. Just how long has it been since you...?"

"None of your business!" she quipped. But Jairus was right. Suddenly she realized that the snack she was going to fix before he called would not satisfy her. She was hungry for something much more satisfying than food. And she was tired of talking about it.

"Thanks for calling, J, but I have to go." Before he could respond, she hung up the phone.

Chapter Three

She was a 36-D. His brain calculated that attribute as soon as she stepped out of the car. Well, that wasn't entirely true. The first thing that registered was her eyes—how large and full of concern they were. Then, being the natural man that he was, his gaze traveled hungrily down to her breasts. He would bet his next paycheck she was a 36-D. His Casanova years had taught him well.

August Knight removed his gloves and began gathering his things to go home.

And there was something else, he thought. Something he couldn't quite identify. Not really an attraction. Attraction was too weak a word. More like involuntary compulsion to be inside her—moving deeply and deliberately.

At first, he thought his testosterone was doing what it did best. But even with the distraction of changing her tire, his sex-Jones made the jeans he wore feel two sizes too small.

August removed his hard hat and wiped his brow with his forearm. A contingent of thick clouds marched across the sky, providing intermittent reprieves from the sun's punishing rays. It had been a good day. The job was on schedule, which kept all of the sidewalk superintendents happy. And he had spent the better part of the day in the air-conditioned cab of the tower crane. His task was to deliver all of the sheet metal required for the tenth floor of the building.

His work was efficient and on point despite the fact that his mind kept conjuring images of Cassandra—undressed and naked wearing only the navy blue pumps from earlier that morning. She would stand wide-legged in front of him, signaling her brash invitation to possess, plunder, and plunge headfirst into her glistening womanhood.

The fantasy always started out the same, with Cassandra daring, audacious, and sassy. But the ending spanned a continuum from tender attention, which brought her to tears, to ravenous ransacking, where both their bodies lay waste—chests heaving and gasping for air. Luckily for him, he worked alone, for the day had been one incessant hard-on. One thing was clear; he would either have to pay his neighbor Maxine a visit tonight or jack off in the shower. Because the bulge in his pants gave new meaning to the words *tension rod.*

Regardless of his lust, August finished the day without mishap or misjudgment. He was good at what he did, and he knew it. Hell, he had practically been born in a construction yard. Thirty-one years ago, amid a loud argument between his mother and father, his mother had gone into labor right on the job site. It was their third child, and the labor went quickly. So quickly that by the time the ambulance arrived, his head was already emerging from her womb. He was born ten minutes later inside the ambulance, which hadn't bothered to leave the curbside.

Since then, the construction yard had been his second home. He had taken odd jobs there as a teenager and began working as a full-time dirt jockey in his mid-twenties. He had never done, or wanted to do, anything else.

So it didn't surprise him when he was able to operate so efficiently while daydreaming so heavily. What he was surprised by was the amount and intensity of his imaginings. Although his encounter with her was brief, Cassandra was running a riot in his mind. And his gut, which was usually accurate when it came to women, told him that he had rocked her world, too.

"Did you pull her?"

August turned toward the voice of Gary Thomas, his apprentice. Charles Edwards, the site manager, was with him.

"Ya know he did," Charles attested. "The only hope the rest of us have is when he's sick, takes a day off, or slides us a hand-me-down."

The laughter of the three coworkers boomed in the air.

"I want all the details on this one," Gary said. "How many moles does she has on her back and does she shave her legs."

Charles put an arm around the other two. "Hell, I want to know how far she takes you in before she gags!"

More laughter.

"Not this time," August responded.

"What!" Charlie and Gary said simultaneously.

Gary was incredulous. "What happened to the Mack-a-roni?"

"Nada. He just won't be seeing Ms. Supra."

"Really?" Gary questioned. "Well you better tell her that."

"Why?" August asked, following the direction of Gary's stare. And the tension he experienced earlier was nothing compared to the hot rush of adrenaline rising up in him now.

Parked in the same place as earlier that morning was Cassandra's white Supra. He watched silently as the door swung slowly open and long, silky legs exited the driver's side.

"What did I tell you?" Charles asked, mesmerized by Cassandra's approach.

Gary's mouth dropped. "Whenever you get done, my brother. Whenever you get done."

She had changed. Her almost-there tank top and barely-there shorts made August divert all his concentration on keeping his Knight stick down—at least for now. Her hair was different, too. It was loose, hanging sleekly against her shoulders. It made him throb. He knew he was obvious. His eyes traveled the length of her body as if they were on vacation. It was blatant, but shit.

"August," she said. "I was hoping you would still be here."

Beside him, Gary and Charles were nudging and throat clearing.

"Cassandra, this is Scrappy Doo and Scooby Dumb, otherwise known as Gary Thomas and Charles Edwards."

The men shook her hand then gave August congratulatory pats on the back. He gave them get-the-hell-out-of-here looks, and they turned to leave.

"Nice meeting you, Cassandra."

"Yeah real nice."

August waited until he and Cassandra were alone before speaking. "Did something happen with your tire?" he asked, knowing damned well that wasn't the case.

"No." She looked away for a moment, then seemed to regroup a bit.

He waited eagerly.

"To tell the truth, I don't know why I'm here, except that some maddening impulse wouldn't let me stay away, and I…"

His kiss was sure and demanding. His tongue went on an exquisite exploration of the inside of her mouth while his hands pulled her at the shoulders. She had never, ever experienced anything so intense. And she had never been so indulgent before. But it was worth it. Already her little man was standing up in the boat and demanding more.

When August released her, his eyes narrowed. At first she mistook it for anger, then recognized it for the lasciviousness that it was—basal, primitive, and everything she needed at that moment. "Let's get out of here," she said.

Moments later they were in her car and accelerating down the expressway. Exhilaration quickened Cassandra's pulse until she wondered exactly how much longer she could contain herself. Judging by the rise in the center of August's pants, they were fighting the same battle.

"This is crazy," she proclaimed, letting the absurdity of the situation intrude upon her need.

"Crazy is good sometimes, Cassandra."

She took her eyes off the road just long enough to watch his lips move—like they were making love to her name.

"Take the next exit."

"What?" she said, realizing that she hadn't been driving toward any particular destination.

"I know a place," he said. "Take this exit" He motioned, and she complied. As they approached the end of the off ramp, she glanced in his direction.

He returned her glance—eyes smoldering. "Take a right."

Again she obliged and turned her car onto Abbott Drive. This corridor of road was always crowded with people on the way to the airport. Today was no exception. They kept a steady pace with the traffic while passing Grants Park and several airport parking lots. And then they came into the part of the city residents called The Strip. It was a six-block area with a cluster of hotels, motels, and car-rental facilities.

"Pick one," August said.

"A hotel?" she questioned.

"Yeah. It's neutral." Then he turned toward her and licked his lips. "And it's naughty."

Her body shivered with the anticipation of being naughty with him.

The multicolored sign in the distance caught her eye. She changed lanes and turned into the entrance of the Crosstown Inn.

"Park on the side," he said.

She pulled into a space to the left of the building. August got out of the car. "I'll be right back."

Cassandra watched as the object of her lust walked into the motel lobby. She turned off the ignition and ran her fingers through her hair.

I am not this hard up, she thought, trying to come to her senses. *For all I know, this man could be crazy or wierd, or Lord knows what else.* Well, the fact that he didn't offer his home told her something. He must be married. *Which means,* she reasoned, *that I must be desperate if I'm willing to sleep with a married man. Is this what my personal life has come to?*

And then she watched him emerge from the entrance, and got that same hot build-up of need she experienced the first time she saw him. It was inevitable that they experience each other body-to-body. She wanted him like she had never wanted anything in her entire life. Papers or no. He would be hers tonight.

"Park in the back," he said, getting into the car, room key in hand. Cassandra started the engine and looked in his direction, a mischievous smile spreading across her face. "You like giving orders, don't you?"

"Yes," he replied.

She drove the car behind the Crosstown Inn and parked. Turning off the motor she studied his ring finger. It was bare and there was no sign of anything having been there. "Are you married?" she asked flatly.

"No."

A tidal wave of relief drenched her coolly. "Then why do I feel like I'm part of a covert operation?"

August closed the passenger door. "You are. I only paid for a single room."

"Why did you do that?" she asked, walking beside him.

"To make it more exciting. Come on." He led her to a rear door and slid the cardkey into the slot. A small green light came on, and he opened the door for her. "Room 308," he said.

They walked up the stairs and down a corridor. Her heart was racing. Room 300. Room 302. I'm really going to do this. Room 304. Room 306. *I guess there is no turning back now.*

They stopped in front of their room. Before sliding the key into the lock, August grabbed her and slid his tongue into her mouth. His lips were searing and possessive, taking from her all hesitation and resistance. The only thing left was a longing, deeply seated and in urgent need of release. He pulled back, stuck the key into the slot, and opened the door.

Inside, the room was dark and stuffy. Cassandra walked over to the air conditioner to turn it on.

"No don't," he said.

"August, it's burning up in here."

"Yes, it is," he responded, and took her in his arms. This time she was ready and returned his kiss with equal fervor. After a few scintillating seconds, she pushed back, dizzy with need.

August stood before her and their eyes locked. He snatched his T-shirt off and threw it on a chair in the corner. Next, he took off his boots and socks. Then slowly he unbuttoned his jeans, and in one swift motion removed his boxers and Levi's.

Cassandra's eyes almost rolled back in her head at the magnificence of his body. His flawless complexion extended from his head to his toes. He had more ripples than any pond she'd ever seen. And every muscle was bulging.

"I'll be right back," he said.

"Where are you going?" she asked, concerned.

"To take a shower."

"No, don't," she said, echoing his words. "I like the way you smell."

A small smile crawled across his lips, and Cassandra began removing her own clothing. In seconds, she stood before him, naked and ablaze with desire.

He took a step toward her and held up his palms. He spread his fingers, and she joined her hands to his. When their hands touched, she was visibly weakened as an electric current passed between them. He took another step toward her. This one closing the gap between them forever. Their naked bodies touching caused low moans from both of their lips. As if on cue, they began a dance that would propel them to the edge of ecstasy and beyond. Their hips ground together, slowly at first. Hinting of the promise of delights to come.

Leisurely August moved downward and upward, pressing himself closer and closer against Cassandra's focal point. She ground her hips to match his movements and found herself panting in anticipation of having him inside her.

Their fingers curled around each other's until they locked together, then he brought his lips crashing down upon hers. His tongue telescoped down into the depths of her soul until she was writhing with desire. Blood surged through her veins, and her womanly juices flowed so freely she feared they would run down the insides of her legs.

She thought his body had been sculpted by Meta Vaux, the famous African-American artist. Marveling at its symmetry and molded structure, she ran her hands slowly over curves and valleys, ridges and high points, soft and firm areas of his torso.

She paused ever so briefly at those places where the sun had made him darker. It was as if she could feel the rays still radiating there. It had been so long since she had experienced a man fully. She was determined to prolong every second.

She could see him watching her in the shadows of the darkened room. His eyes narrowed to slits, his breathing heavy. *Is this what its like to really touch a man,* she wondered, not remembering it being this mesmerizing or hypnotic.

Perspiration dampened their skin, and her hunger for him increased. She pressed her lips against his chest and heard his intake of breath. *Is that how a man responds,* she asked herself. Wanting more, Cassandra let her tongue continue exploring where her hands left off. August was salty yet at the same time intoxicatingly sweet. When her lips found a nipple and sucked it, his resulting moan made her ravenous for more.

She continued her journey of tasting and savoring him. His skin was a dizzy mixture of soap and the day's work. Her own nipples ripened like fresh fruit. Their hardening made her moan.

As if he could no longer be content to just stand, August began his own exploration, sucking her neck and thumbing her nipples at

103

the same time. The sensation was so pure and exquisite, she bit her lip to keep from crying out.

Aside from their frenzied panting, there were no other sounds in the room. Neither of them could speak. They could only do the things to each other that had plagued their minds for hours.

Without warning he lifted her and placed her on the bed. The sheets were slightly cooler than the room temperature. Tiny goose bumps broke out on her skin.

August retrieved a condom from his pants pocket and returned to her on the bed. He quickly put it on, and with one deep thrust, he plunged into the moist recesses of her womanhood. And just as quickly he brought himself all the way out. After what seemed like an eternity, he continued in this manner—thrusting in and pulling out; thrusting in and pulling out. Each time, he would make her wait for his next invasion into her. She pulled at his body, arched her back, and begged for the return of his rock-hard penis. But his teasing continued. Cassandra must have died a thousand times between each plunge into her sopping center. But every return was a sensation off the Richter scale.

Then something in the rhythm of their joining made them lose control. All at once their thrusts toward each other were more forceful and unconstrained. They were riding each other into paradise, swept up into a current of urgency. They pulled, clawed, scratched, grunted, and damn near howled in their frenzy. In her blinding need to reach fulfillment, Cassandra rolled over onto August and slid herself up and down his stiffness. With each rise and fall of her hips, she rubbed her clit against his body and tightened her muscles around him.

She could smell the scent of their joining, and it intensified her need. Sweat marinated their bodies in the sweltering room. His hands reached up to finger her nipples, which had hardened into small pebbles. Then he pushed dark tips of her mammaries together and drew them both into his mouth. A warm river of wetness awaited them along with August's eager tongue, which flicked across the ultra-sensitive areas. And then he sucked her breasts rhythmically until she felt the beginnings of a scream forming in her throat.

She rode him hard, and soon he added his moans to her own. And then a sensation of hot fury consumed them both. It started at their loins and spread out swiftly to all other parts of their bodies. Together, in Room 308 of the Crosstown Inn, two strangers splintered into a million parts of themselves, and then became one golden explosion.

Chapter Four

When Cassandra got within a mile of the construction site, the area between her legs began to throb. Her femininity had a mind all its own, she decided, noting the way it responded to being within close proximity to August. After their furied exchange, she had taken him back to the construction site and gone home a new woman. A new horny woman.

She had tossed and turned all night—crazy with desire. Finally, she stuffed a pillow between her legs in an effort to trick herself into believing that August was there. When she awoke, there was a wet spot on her panties and on the pillow. Her woman-scent was strong with need.

An extralong shower, and Cassandra emerged clean, fresh, and ready for the day. Or so she thought. Now, nearing the site, the randy feelings from the night before were re-awakening. And she feared the rest of her day would be lost without a good dose of August's prowess to tide her over.

"Meet me here tomorrow," he had said after taking her body to the edge once more. His head was still buried between her legs. His lips glistened with she-juice, and like an answer to a prayer, he licked them ever so seductively.

"August, I..."

"Don't say no," he said. With his mouth so close to her, his words vibrated her clit and made her shiver.

Needing his expert guidance to ecstasy again like she needed her next breath, she stroked his head and said, "One more time, August. Please."

He pushed her legs gently apart. She could feel his breath warming her soft, pink opening. "Will you come?" he asked, lips brushing against lips.

"Yes," she proclaimed as the sensation detonated pulsing spasms within her. When his tongue finally entered her, she was already tumbling over the edge.

"Sssss, oh, August," she screamed, and collapsed back against the bed.

There it is, she thought passing the Brookhaven billboard. At first glance, she saw no sign of him, and was almost relieved. Perhaps her throbbing would subside, and she could make it through the day.

And then she saw him giving hand signals to someone operating a crane. He glanced at his watch and then out at the road. Their eyes locked for a brief second, and Cassandra turned back to the expressway. The throbbing increased, and she knew it was going to be a very long day.

She hadn't worn her black Versace suit in years. She was glad to discover that it still fit. And under it, she wore a surprise for August. She had dusted off some of her best Victoria's Secret lingerie. Yesterday's slap and tickle reminded Cassandra of the sexual being she was. It also reminded her that she had only just met August. Seeing him again tonight could be a big mistake. As she entered the building, she realized she needed advice.

She walked quickly and deliberately down the hall and into Jairus Flemming's office. He looked away from his spreadsheet program and dropped his jaw to his chin.

"Good lawd," he said.

"What?" she asked, standing in front of his desk.

"First of all, your lips are swollen. Second, the last time you wore that suit you were dating that nightclub owner, Jimmy."

"Johnny," she corrected.

"Yeah whatever. And third, it's a good thing your name's not Victoria. Cause you sure can't keep a secret. Now which ensemble are you wearing under that, the midnight blue or the Egyptian purple?"

Jairus sat back in his leather chair smug as ever.

"Alright!" she said, taking a seat opposite him. "Am I that obvious?"

"Only to me, darlin'." Jairus got up and closed the door to his office. He knew their discussion needed to be private. "So, you saw him after all?"

"Umm-hmm."

"By the look on your face, you enjoyed yourself."

"Umm-hmm."

"But?" Contrary to the look of contentment in her face, he could tell that something was bothering her.

"But I'm not sure if I should keep seeing him."

"Why not?"

"Because. I don't know anything about him."

"You know how he makes you feel."

Cassandra took a deep breath. "Better than I've ever felt in my entire life."

Jairus' concerned expression was taken over by a frown. "Better than me?" he asked, with a puppy-dog look..

At first, she didn't respond. Then slowly she nodded her head affirmatively.

"Daaamn!" he said, rubbing his chin. "Then maybe you shouldn't see him."

"Why?" Cassandra asked, sitting forward.

"Because...it sounds like you're letting one evening cloud your judgment."

She couldn't believe what she was hearing. "Nonsense. I'm one of the most level headed people you know."

"Yeah. When it comes to business."

"But when it comes to men?" she asked, defensiveness elevating her voice.

"But when it comes to men, you think with Miss Muffin rather than your head."

Miss Muffin was the pet name they had used for her private part.

The very reason they had named it was because it seemed to be the third person in their relationship. Whatever Miss Muffin wanted Miss Muffin got. And back then, Miss Muffin wanted all Jairus had to offer. Their lovemaking surpassed anything she had experienced, until now.

"Where are you now?" he asked, sensing her departure from their conversation.

"In his arms," she said, getting up from the chair. "That settles it. I'm meeting him tonight." She turned and opened his office door. "Thanks, J," she said, and headed off to her office.

August used the radio to tell Gary it was time for lunch. The kid had done all right in the driver's seat that morning. Of course it took him longer to move the wall than if he had done it himself, but Gary was in training.

He walked over to his truck and opened the passenger-side door where a small cooler kept his lunch from the heat. He removed three tuna sandwiches, a bottle of Power Ade, and a large plum. He turned the deep-red object in his hand and thought of Cassandra's delicate fruit, and how he had plucked it wantonly and without regret. He found it hard to believe that a woman that beautiful would surrender herself to him so completely. But she had. And he was grateful.

"Hey August, we're going to Wendy's. You wanna tag along?"

"Naw. Thanks though."

The group passed on the way to Charles' van. August knew that most of the crew referred to him as The Lone Ranger. He earned that nickname partly because being a tower crane operator requires that you work mostly alone. The other part was due to the fact that he was a loner and a man of few words. That suited him just fine. But it was the demise of many a relationship with women. That's why he enjoyed his neighbor Maxine. They provided each other with the means to relieve themselves from nature's strong urges. But they weren't a couple and made no demands on each other's time or attention.

Until last night, he could have gone on like that for quite a while. But Cassandra...she was a different kind of release. What he had shared with her...his body had felt things he didn't know it could feel. And he wanted more. He had to have more.

"I should have gotten her number!" he declared, after taking a gulp of the blue liquid. He had tried to prevent himself from thinking about it all morning, but the dreadful possibility existed that she wouldn't show up tonight. He could be number who-knows-what out of the many men she's had and cast aside like old newspapers. Hell, he had done it to women enough times in his life. But so far, he had never been on the receiving end.

He unwrapped the foil around sandwich number three. "What goes around comes around, I guess."

He thought back to earlier that morning. He had been giving Gary directions for operating the crane and at the same time checking for a white Supra on the expressway. After taking his eyes off the crane several times, he returned to work, only to find his mind demanding one last look. So he took it, and there she was. And she appeared to be searching the yard for him until they made eye contact. He couldn't read the expression on her face. He didn't know if it was disappointment or relief. But he knew one thing. He was glad to see her.

She could have taken another route to work, he mused. She didn't have to come this way. Unless she wanted to rub it in my face, a darker voice in his thoughts suggested. After finishing off his lunch, August realized that he would just have to resign himself to the fact that last night's exploits may have been a one-time thing.

I really should have gotten her phone number, he thought.

Chapter Five

The day progressed without incident. *It's amazing what good sex will do,* Cassandra thought as she checked off the final item on her task list. She closed her day planner and zipped the leather binder closed. She had taken on the day in a way she had almost forgotten was possible. The fire was slowly returning to her passion for the industry, and the old Cassandra Hearst was coming back with a vengeance.

"Ms. Hearst?" Larry entered her office in his usual perfunctory manner. He was the most efficient assistant she had ever had. He always did as he was told, and without complaint. Even when she turned into the high-powered, fast-talking bitch that she was sometimes known for, she never once heard him grumble. She had often wondered what lay beneath that wonderfully accommodating exterior Larry presented.

"Yes, Larry," she said, glancing up.

"Do you have time to review a proposal for next month's diversity project?"

The wall clock read 4:55. Her rendezvous with August was at 5:30. It would probably take her all of ten minutes to read the proposal. She would still have enough time to get to the motel by 5:30 or shortly thereafter.

"Sure," she said, taking the file. Inside was a five-page proposal for activities for company employees to participate in to help them achieve the firm's goals for an inclusive organization. One of the first orders of business when Cassandra became CEO was to champion a company-wide diversity initiative. After three years, the results were promising, and DirectData was being studied by other businesses as a model of success in the area of cultural awareness.

After looking over the proposal, Cassandra made a few recommendations and signed her name at the bottom. As she did so, a soft disturbance started in her lower abdomen and traveled down to her toes. Within seconds she recognized it as eagerness for August's body, and suddenly she couldn't wait to get to the motel.

Quickly she shut her computer down, put the last of the remaining files in her desk drawer, and headed out of her office. With proposal in hand, she stopped at Larry's desk to return it.

"Have a good evening, Ms. Hearst," he said, with what seemed to Cassandra like a knowing smile. She paused for a second while placing the document in the in box on his desk. Was she mistaking the look on his face? It couldn't have been more smug if he had been a fly on the wall during the heat of her lust-driven exchange with August. And then the flash of secret knowledge was gone, and he looked like good ol' Larry again.

"Good night, Larry," she said.

Maneuvering through the city of cubicles, she was shocked to see some of the employees glance up from their desks and give her strangely discerning smiles. *They know,* she thought quickening her pace. Was her business Item One in the daily electronic newsletter she wondered? And then a shadowy thought ruined her mood. What if word got out that the CEO of DirectData was getting her jollies on with a construction worker in a cheap motel? It might tarnish her career. Exiting the building she realized that she couldn't take that chance.

The clock on the dashboard read 6:15. Damn. The things he endured for a good lay. *I can't believe you're still here, Buddy-O. Was it*

113

that good? Rubbing his throbbing maleworks, he realized that yes, it was that good. He was actually supposed to be on the yard now, but he had convinced the site manager to let him take what he claimed was a much-needed break. He had agreed to come back later on that night or early the next morning to finish the job.

Maybe she had an accident? Or another blowout? August shifted in the driver's seat of his tan Chevy Suburban. *Maybe she got what she was after and has moved on, leaving me like a whipped puppy sniffing for remnants of her scent. Good thing I'm pile driving on Thursday,* he thought. *By then I'll have some serious tension to work off.*

To keep himself cool, he had kept the truck running and air conditioner on full blast. Not so much from the heat, but from the anticipation of tasting Cassandra again. August put the large truck in reverse.

"Too bad. We could have been great for each other's bodies," he said, about to back out of the parking space. Then in his rearview mirror, he saw a glint of white. His heart thrummed wildly in his chest. It was Cassandra.

She parked in nearly the same spot as before and stepped out of her car. Cautiously, she looked around, and her eyes settled onto his as he emerged from his truck. Steady, Buddy-O, he reprimanded as he felt the blood rushing to his private. The suit she donned looked painted on, and something about her walk made him wonder what she was wearing underneath.

"I'm sorry I'm late. I just..."

"It's alright. Come on."

He lead her to the back, and together they entered the building.

"You already got the room?" she asked.

"Yeah," he said, walking briskly through the hallway. "Down here."

"What if I hadn't shown up?"

His adrenaline was charging through his veins. "Then you would have missed out on the best sex of your life."

He stopped at Room 228, and in seconds they were inside and in each other's arms.

They kissed each other as if there was no quenching their desire.

Their clothes came tumbling off and down they dropped onto the bed consumed with an overwhelming need to mate. August kissed her mouth, all the while his fingers searched frantically for her opening. Once found, he donned a condom and plunged himself deeply inside her.

Their pace was hectic. August ran his hands along the sides of her thighs, raising first one leg and then the other. He groaned deeply as he descended farther and farther into the depths of her innermost space. She matched him thrust for thrust, nearly angry that she couldn't get closer to him than this. The movement of their bodies thickened the heat in the room. Sweat poured off August like summer rain.

His breathing became more audible as did hers. Soon the room was filled with the moans of their hard ride to heaven.

"Umm!"

"Aah!"

"Come with me," he said, as a thousand rockets lifted him to the sky. Only seconds behind him, Cassandra's climax shattered her from the inside out.

August tumbled to Cassandra's side, chest heaving. Her breaths were equally labored.

"Oh God," she said.

He swiped at the sweat trickling down his temples. "I don't think God had much to do with it."

"What do you mean?" she asked, letting her head fall in his direction.

"I mean that was deliciously sinful."

August didn't look at her. He stared straight up at the ceiling. Cassandra thought it was just as well. Getting too comfortable with each other would make their liaisons more than what they were— plain and simple sexual encounters. No mus no fuss, she thought , remembering her earlier hesitation.

"I almost stayed away," she said.

August's suspicions were confirmed.

"When I left work, I sat in the company parking lot for half an hour wondering what I should do," she continued. "And I'm not normally an indecisive person."

He folded his arms behind his head. "So what made you come?"

"I wanted to tell you to your face that I wasn't going to continue our, our..."

"But you did."

"Yes," she admitted, trying to discern what he found so compelling above them.

"Do you regret it?" he asked.

Cassandra drew a deep breath. "No."

"Good," he said turning over. He draped a muscular arm over her. "Cause there's plenty more where that came from." He positioned himself closer and took possession of her mouth. Their tongues found each other and mingled in a dance of heightening desire. August hadn't felt this virile since he was nineteen, he thought, noticing the stiffening in his loins.

He slid himself on top of her and rolled his hips on hers. She responded in kind and matched his motions.

"I want you," he said, passion deepening his voice.

"August," she murmured in protest.

"I want you," he repeated. "Like this...tomorrow...and the next day...and the next."

She wanted to resist, but the heat between her legs wouldn't let her. "Please," she said, and her own voice betrayed her. Instead of being an objection, it came out sounding like a plead.

She gasped feeling his full erection on her. August did a swift change of Trojans and slid himself easily inside as she was still soaked from a few moments ago.

Cassandra was nearly paralyzed with pleasure. He pushed himself into her with such force, she could hardly contain herself. She felt the inevitable buildup of her release.

"No, not yet," she said into his ear.

"Let me feel it," he whispered back.

The sound of his words propelled her forward into the abyss. Her muscles contracted strongly and rhythmically against his organ.

"Ah, ah," he said, as he continued pumping madly into her damp lovenest. "Ah!" he growled, as he was catapulted into orbit.

Chapter Six

August took a matchbook from an ashtray and wrote something inside the cover.

"Here" he said, handing it to Cassandra.

"What's this?" she asked, taking the promotional item for Crosstown Inn.

"It's my cell phone number." And for the first time since they'd met, he held her gaze for a long time. "In case you need to reach me for whatever reason." He shrugged and pulled on his T-shirt. They were both fully dressed and ready to go after having one more taste of each other in the shower.

Cassandra had to admit that she was disappointed that he had to return to work. Her body could stand another dose of his hard and heavy humping. But his phone number? Now that was a different matter.

"Let's not turn this into something that it isn't." she said.

"Look, I'm not offering you roses or anything. It's just my number…in case you get lonely in the night."

Her eyebrow arched. "Are you saying you're available for booty calls?"

He bound her up in his arms. "I'm saying that there's a chemistry between us. Now, I'm no expert, but shit like this doesn't come around too often. So while it's here..."

"I know," she said, and dropped the matchbook into her purse.

The next morning, Cassandra sat in her wood-paneled office flipping the matchbook back and forth between her fingers. For the past two days, her thoughts had been consumed by August. This day was no exception.

"Well," Jairus said, startling her out of her silence.

"Geez, I didn't even hear you come in."

He took a seat opposite her. "I see."

She waited for the game of twenty questions to begin. After a few moments of silence, she realized that he wasn't going to prompt her. She sat forward, closing her hand around August's phone number.

"You know me. I've always thought that a good night's sleep was better than sex. No offense, J."

He cocked his head slightly to the right. "None taken."

"But this thing with August, it's...it's..."

"August? His name is August? August what?"

Cassandra shrugged. "I don't know his last name."

Jairus sat back against the chair, his expression bewildered. "You're giving this man the best that you've got, and you don't even know his last name? Are you sure that's wise?"

"It just never came up, that's all."

"Geez, Cassandra. I don't know..."

"You don't have to know. This is my life, remember?"

He shook his head. A smile of amusement took over his face. "Alright, already. Don't get your panties in a wad." And then his smile faded into a mischievous grin. He leaned forward. "Besides, that's August's job."

Without thinking, Cassandra hurled the matchbook she'd been

holding. It tagged him on the shoulder and bounced to the ground near his feet. "Ow," he said faking injury. He picked up the matchbook and read the cover. "Crosstown Inn? Uh-huh."

"Uh-huh, nothing," she said.

He flipped the cardboard object open. "August, 555-5218."

"Give me that," she said, extending her hand across her desk.

"No," he said, clutching it to his chest.

Cassandra got up, determined to retrieve her memento. "I'm not playing with you."

She reached for it. The matchbook disappeared within Jairus's large hand. "I said no."

"I'm warning you!" She grabbed wildly at his closed fist. He held his long arm up and swung it out of her reach. She lunged for his hand and in doing so, lost her balance. "Damn you!" she said, toppling into him. Her momentum knocked Jairus backward, and they both tumbled to the floor.

She landed squarely on top of him, and the two warring factions grinned as laughter overtook them. Cassandra's hair fell lightly into Jairus's face, and he brushed it away in a gesture that seemed to have been with them since the beginning of time. Their laughter subsided, and for one long second, their eyes caught.

How often had their bodies been like this, she wondered. A hundred, a thousand times?

She still feels good, he admitted to himself.

Cassandra felt a familiar wave of emotion approaching. It came slowly from a million miles away. She could feel his breath on her lips and a familiar stiffening in his crotch. It was one of the longest moments in her life.

"I think we better get up from here," he said.

"Of course," she replied, and stood.

Jairus got up and handed her the matchbook. He gave her a sweet kiss on the forehead. "Call him," he said, and walked out of her office.

"Is everything alright, Ms. Hearst?" Larry asked, rushing through the door?

Cassandra straightened the toppled chair. "Everything's fine, Larry. Just fine."

But she didn't call August that day. Or the next, or the next. She kept busy with her work, took cold showers, and got up two hours earlier so she could take another route in to the office. She held her rescheduled meeting with Van Housen and Associates, and was so impressed with their presentation she offered them a consulting assignment with the company. And despite all that, the memory of August thrusting inside her burned like liquid fire.

"Are you smoking again?" Larry asked one day when she was absentmindedly opening and closing the cover of the matchbook.

"Of course not!" she snapped.

"Sorry," he said, picking up her outgoing mail. "I didn't mean to upset you."

Larry whisked himself out of her office before she could offer him an apology.

This is ridiculous, she thought. *I'm torturing myself!*

Cassandra pulled her sports car into the parking lot of Sherick's, one of Minneapolis' upscale restaurants in the downtown area. She exited the car quickly after parking, eager for her monthly luncheon meeting with Twin Cities 100, a community service group where she was on the board of directors.

As she approached the establishment, a greeter opened the door and held it for her. "Welcome to Sherick's."

"Thank you," Cassandra responded, removing her Ray Bans and

placing them into a soft eel-skin case. She looked around, slowly giving her eyes the time they needed to adjust to the subdued lighting in the restaurant. The dark wood paneling made for an even darker ambience.

Jautily, she walked up to the host station. The woman behind the post looked just out of her teens. "Table for one?" she asked with a broad smile.

"No, I'm meeting a group for lunch. The name…"

Before she could finish her sentence, she heard a blast of laughter from around the corner. Then the sound diminished into a cacophony of voices she recognized. She returned the hostess' smile.

"Never mind. I can find them."

She walked around the corner into the west dining area and seated in one of the private rooms, were five of the Twin Cities 100 board of directors.

Cassandra felt her chest swell with pride. It always did when she was with her friends. It did her heart such a tremendous world of good each time she saw a group of highly successful African-American women together in one place.

"You made it," Sheena said. She and her husband Rick Haynes owned Sherick's.

"Sorry, I'm late. My staff meeting ran long."

"That's alright," said Lorene Matheson, the vice president. "We haven't ordered yet."

Paula Johnson, the secretary, elbowed Cassandra. "We've been too busy admiring girlfriend's new ring."

Cassandra followed everyone's eyes to the hand of Simone Winters, the president of the organization. On the ring finger of Simone's left hand sat the largest diamond Cassandra had ever seen.

"Wow!" Cassandra exclaimed, taking the woman's hand. "It's absolutely exquisite. Did you and Harvey renew your wedding vows?"

Simone licked her lips. "Not exactly."

Jamika West, Twin Cities' lawyer smiled wistfully at Simone.

"Tell her how you got it."

Another blast of laughter erupted in the establishment.

"You ladies are having way too much fun here," the waiter said, approaching Cassandra. "Can I get you something to drink, ma'am?"

"Water with lemon, thank you."

"Certainly. I'll be right back."

"Now what's so funny?" Cassandra asked, looking from friend to friend then finally settling her gaze on Simone.

"Well..." Simone began.

"And this time, don't leave out any of the juicy parts," Sheena admonished, chuckling.

Simone shifted slightly in her chair and then leaned forward. "Last week, my secretary came into the office wearing a diamond ring on her finger the size of Algeria."

"What?"

"Girl, it looked like she needed a sling for her arm, that rock was so heavy. So, I asked her how she got it."

"What did she say?"

"She said..." And then Simone made a fist with her hand and moved it up and down near her mouth.

This time Cassandra's loud laughter joined the rest. "You're kidding!"

Simone shook her head. "That was my response. But she was serious. Apparently she gave her boyfriend the best head he's ever had in his life. So, I thought, shit...I want a ring like that."

"Don't we all!" Jamika responded.

Simone chuckled. "So I went home early that day. I called my sister and had her come and get the kids. Then I put fresh sheets on the bed, took a shower, and put on one of my Frederick's of Hollywood numbers."

"Ooh, no you didn't."

"Yes I did. And when Donte came home, I had a Polaroid picture of me in the teddy pinned on the wall in the entryway. I put a note on it that said, 'The real thing is waiting for you upstairs.'"

"You are too much."

"Wait, I haven't gotten to the good part yet. Donte likes to watch me do myself, so as soon as I heard him pull up in the driveway, I started playin' with myself, that way I'd be good and juicy by the time he got upstairs." Simone lowered her voice. "When he walked into the bedroom and saw me in the middle of getting myself off, he dropped his briefcase, his jacket, and his thang shot up like a rocket."

"Dang, girl."

"You said not to leave out any of the details."

As horny as Cassandra had been for the past few days, she couldn't wait to hear the rest. "And then what happened?"

"He just stood there watching. Every now and then he would say things like, 'Damn, Simone' and 'Oh, shit!' After I came, I told him to take his clothes off, because I wanted to do him next."

"Would you ladies like to start with an appetizer?"

"No!" they all said, mesmerized by Simone's story.

"We'll call you when we're ready to order," Cassandra said. The waiter left without another word.

"So then," Simone continued, leaning in even farther and lowering her voice a bit more, "he took his clothes off so fast, all I could see was a blur and then he was naked."

The women whooped and nudged one another playfully.

"So I sat him in a chair and got on my knees in front of him."

Cassandra remembered August being in a similar position in front of her and suddenly she could feel herself moistening at the thought.

"When I touched him, he felt harder than the diamond I wanted, but I went down on him nice and slow."

"Umm," Sheena said.

"At first I pretended it was a Fudgesicle like I always do. Then I remembered what my secretary said, and my mouth closed around him like a Kirby vacuum."

Paula chuckled. "You are too much!"

"Girl, Donte thought so, too. Pretty soon, he started wiggling and whimpering. And I never have been one to take him in all the way. My husband is rather large. But the more I thought about that ring, the more of him I took. The next thing I knew, his hands were on my head and his toes were curling!"

Cassandra knew that feeling all too well. Larry's Tongue Teaser had had the same effect on her. Thinking about it, it was if someone had turned off the air conditioning in the room and turned on the furnace.

"By the time I finished, I had his balls in my mouth, too and Donte was babbling something I couldn't even understand. We hadn't had sex in few days so when he finally came, he shot his hot semen straight into the back of my throat. I swallowed loud and hard so he could hear me."

"Uh, uh, uh."

"The next day, I asked him to take me shopping, and that's when I got this." Simone held up her hand.

The women at the table howled with laughter. During the rest of their luncheon, there were periodic jibes at Simone regarding her ring. Cassandra tried hard to focus on the meeting and her food, but she found her mind wandering to August and what he might be willing to do if she made his toes curl.

Chapter Seven

It had been a long day on the yard, and it was only just past lunch. Gary hadn't been doing so well, and August was starting to get irritated and impatient.

"What do you mean, why am I on the radio! I'm on the radio because you can't keep the hand signals straight." August stared straight up where his apprentice sat in the cab of a crane—lowering a steel girder on to the newly built twelfth floor. August held his breath as the kid pulled off the job, but just barely.

"Come on down from there. I'll take over from here."

He waited—pacing for Gary to return to the ground. *What's with this kid*, he wondered. *Even more importantly, what's with me?* All morning he had been moody and eruptive.

Gary approached, looking tense and frustrated. "You got beef with me?"

"Hell yeah, I got beef with you! That's a crane, you greenhorn, not a Tonka truck. And when you're dealing with anything on the yard, especially cranes, safety is numero uno, you got that!"

"Yeah, I got it."

"You gotta be alert at all times. Not all the time, but all the time! You have the vantage point because you're up so high. Take advantage of that. You have to be sharp and frosty always. You understand?"

"I'm sorry, man, I just got a little distracted."

"Look, kid, if you're careless, and you hurt somebody, an apology ain't gonna mean shit. Now, I know it feels like I'm coming down hard on you, but that's life on the yard. Can you hang?"

"I can hang."

"Good, now watch my smoke," August said, heading off toward the large crane. When his cell phone rang, he got a split-second rush of hope that it might be Cassandra. And then he shoved it away. His other calls had been disappointments, this one would be, too. If she hadn't called by now, she wasn't going to. Best to get on with life.

He flipped the phone open. "Yeah."

"August," she said in a voice so hot, he could feel it through the receiver.

"Dark Lady," he returned and stopped in his tracks.

"So, you've nicknamed me?"

"Yes."

"Ummm," Cassandra purred. "I like it."

"I'm glad." His pants started to feel a bit snug. "To what do I owe the honor of your call?"

"I just wanted to tell you what I'm doing."

"What?" he asked in a voice barely above a whisper.

"I'm laying down."

"Yes…"

"Naked."

"Yes…"

"In Room 200 of the Crosstown Inn."

"Oh God."

"I don't think God had much to do with it. What I need is positively sinful. Can you come now?"

"If I'm not there in fifteen minutes, you can start without me."

August closed the phone and slid it back into its holder. He walked over to Gary and slapped him on the back. "Gary, I'm not feeling so good. If I talk to Charles, will you finish up here?"

Gary's face lit up. "Sure!"

"And you'll remember what I said?" he asked, walking toward the yard office.

"I'll remember."

Good, he thought, turning his fast walk into a trot.

Thirteen and a half minutes later, there was a knock on the door ... Room 200 in the Crosstown Inn.

"August?"

"It's me, baby."

"It's open."

True to her word, Cassandra was lying on the bed, disrobed and horny. Just the sight of him stepping through the door hardened her nipples in anticipation of their sex. He started to undress, and her arousal became almost more than she could bear.

"I tried to stay away," she said, swerving her hips.

"I tried not to think about you," he responded, removing his shoes and pants.

"I took cold showers," she whispered, running her hands across her breasts and down between her legs.

"I jacked off," he responded, freeing himself from his boxers and standing naked before her.

"But see," she said, sliding a finger inside herself. When she pulled it out, it was dripping wet.

He went to her then. Kneeling down on the side of the bed he took her damp finger and brought it into his mouth. Cassandra moaned as his warm tongue swirled around it and brought it out clean.

"There's more where that came from," she said, opening her legs to him. He descended hungrily upon her. His tongue danced in and out of her—and she rocked her hips toward him, desperate for the explosion she needed so badly. His tongue flicked quickly over her clit, and Cassandra's pleasure was audible.

"Ooh yes. Yes, baby. Ah-ow. Szzzz."

When she came, she was screaming so loudly, she thought the employees at DirectData could hear her.

August rose from his prone position and Cassandra gasped. His penis was so large and engorged, it looked like it would burst. Quickly, he climbed on top of her. She grabbed his male member, sheathed it in a condom, and inserted it into herself. And August moved with a rhythm that whirled them both like a hurricane.

His deep-set eyes bored down into hers. "Did you miss me?" he asked, riding fast.

Cassandra arched her back, barely able to think. "Yes," she whimpered.

"I can't hear you," he said, riding her faster, harder.

"Yes!" she responded, barely aware of herself or her surroundings.

All that mattered was this feeling between her legs, spreading out and taking her over. All that mattered…

He had one of her legs now. Pulling it up. "I missed you too, Cassandra. Ah-ah, I m-missed…"

One super-hard thrust, and she could feel him spilling himself inside her. And somewhere, in that same place, she burst open like a new star.

"I can't believe I took off work for this."

"Hey!" she punched him in the ribs.

"No, don't misunderstand. It was worth it, definitely. I've just never done anything like this before."

"I know what you mean. I'm usually a stickler when it comes to my job."

"Really? Where do you work?

"DirectData."

"I imagined you had one of those corporate cushy jobs. But what do you do?"

She swallowed. "I run the place."

August whistled through is teeth.

"Is that a problem?"

He turned to her. "Not for me, unless..." Worry lines emerged at his temples.

"Unless what?" she asked, concerned.

"Unless word gets out." He smoothed out the hairs of his moustache. "If the yard crew gets wind of this, they'll label me a greaser for sure."

"A greaser."

"Yeah. It means flunky."

So, I'm not the only one who has a problem with people finding out, she thought.

"I know what you mean. Imagine the reverse of that, and that's what people would think about me."

He brushed a stray curl back from the side of her face. "So, it's a secret then?"

"Yes. My lips are sealed."

"Oh?" he responded with a kiss. In seconds her lips parted and their tongues mingled eagerly, then Cassandra pushed back.

"Do you have to go back to work tonight?"

"Yes."

Disappointment clouded her soft brown eyes.

"But not to work. Just to inspect someone else's." August propped himself up on his elbow. "Come with me?" He smiled.

"To the construction site?"

"We won't be there long. An hour, tops. And then we can come back here."

After a quick shower and change back into their clothes, they were off to the construction site. Once there, they entered the office.

August put on his hard hat and then handed one to Cassandra.

"Here, put this on."

She took the hat and placed it on her head. It was way too big and came down so far, it nearly covered her eyes. She pushed up the top of the hat with the back of her hand.

"How do I look?"

August had never been one to mince words. "Like you've just had some damn good sex."

They laughed, and he took her hand. "This way," he said.

He grabbed a flashlight on the way out, and together they walked across the yard. It was quiet, and their feet made scuffing sounds in the dirt. August helped Cassandra maneuver around steel beams, bulldozers, and mounds of sand.

They stopped at a place where monstrous steel beams stood at attention on floor after floor of new construction. August shined a light straight up at the west end of the structure. He squinted to see better.

"Ah, this is no good. I'm gonna have to go up."

"Go up where?"

"There," he said, pointing to the crane in the distance. He smiled. "That's the place I run."

Cassandra took in the massive piece of machinery. If it had skin, it would look like some huge dinosaur. Perhaps Godzilla or a brontosaurus Rex. Should couldn't imagine what it would take to make that thing move and do what you want it to do. The thought of August commanding the steel beast warmed her—made her hot.

He walked toward it. "Stay here," he said. "I'll be right back."

His strides were long and powerful. It took her some effort to catch up to him. "Let me come with you," she said.

His heart pounded, and he licked his lips. "I could get fired for this," he said, putting his arm around her. Together they climbed up to the top of the crane and entered the cab. It was a tight fit, but they both managed to sit inside.

"OK," he said, pushing a few buttons and levers. The cab turned toward the largest part of the city.

Cassandra's eyes took in the spectacular view. She could see for miles. The downtown area looked ablaze with lights. The colors of the buildings were swept up in the darkness, leaving row upon row of tall, thin shadows with twinkling lights.

"It's magical, August."

"We sometimes have to work at night, but I usually don't mind. When it's clear, like it is tonight, sitting up here is like touching heaven."

Cassandra leaned forward, dazzled by the nightscene.

He watched her, intrigued. "You're a brave sister. I've had trainees up here nervous and flighty, wanting to get back down to the ground after only a few minutes of being up here.

She looked at him. "Most of it is you. I feel safe with you." She returned her gaze to the skyline. "And the rest is simply beauty. It has a way of taking away fear."

He thought about that. And then on impulse he pulled her into his arms. They exchanged a heated kiss. Seconds later, Cassandra was unbuttoning his jeans. He watched intently as she worked fervently to free him from his trousers. When she had accomplished her task, she smiled slyly at him and then down at his stiffening erection.

"Now what, pray tell, are you going to do with that?" he asked.

The answer came in the moist recesses of her mouth. He gasped at her bold assault. The feeling was so exquisite, August slammed his hands against the side of the cab. He clutched and clawed his fingers across the metal interior.

"Damn, it's good, baby," he said.

Then, settling into her attentions, he pulled his hands from the walls and removed her hard hat to run his fingers though the corkscrew curls of her hair. His hands lowered and raised with her head as her motions glided him strongly into the altitude surrounding them. As her hand cupped and worked his balls, a determined tongue placed a steady stream of tongue flicks across the thick vein of his penis.

Then remembering Simone's story, she slid her lips tightly from the base to the tip. "Ummm," she moaned.

Cassandra closed her eyes, feeling the inevitable rise in temperature, the ridged throbbing of the impending eruption. She smiled inwardly, liking the feeling of control over August's sexual destiny. Before he came, she stopped and executed a quick teasing work with her tongue that made August cry out and clutch frantically again at the cab walls.

She wanted to treat him to the same advance-and-retreat sensations that had left her trembling weakly beneath him. Her wanton mouth traversed boldly up and down the length of him, pausing long enough to pay special attention to his balls, which were warm and soft between her teeth. The rush of pleasuring him, of feeling his moans was doing her body good. She could feel herself approaching the edge.

She moaned working him again. Taking everything he had to offer. August looked out into the night. Through the cab window he could see the moon hanging low in the sky and the stars surrounding it. He felt himself rocketing toward those stars. At last he closed his eyes as his soul detonated into space.

Cassandra found herself falling, falling. And when he released himself to her, she was also surrendering—overcome by the night and the sky, and the man who had made her lose all control.

"You know," she said, as he stroked her hair, "I've had my mouth on every inch of your body, and I don't even know your last name."

"Hmmm," he responded.

She turned from her cozy space nestled between his legs. "What's that supposed to mean?"

"It means that maybe what we have right now is comfortable." He smiled and looked ten years younger. "Besides, if I tell you my last name, the next thing you know, you'll be inviting me to your house or something."

She liked his game and decided to play along.

"If you tell me your last name, I'll invite you to my house. "It was out before she could think better of it. Now she'd really stepped in it.

Maybe he won't go there, she thought. Maybe...

"Knight," he said. "My last name is Knight."

Well there it is, she mused, feeling slightly apprehensive and obligated to reciprocate.

"Mine's Hearst."

She didn't think it was possible, but his smile broadened. "Nice to meet you, Ms. Hearst."

A flash of their earlier exchange dazzled her mind.

"The pleasure is all mine, Mr. Knight."

Chapter Eight

"Miss Hearst," Larry said, poking his head in her office doorway.

"Yes, Larry."

"There's someone here to see you. A Mr. Knight."

Cassandra was up and out of her chair before she realized it. The look of surprise on Larry's face told her how ridiculous she must have seemed bolting up like that. *Settle down, hot momma,* she told herself. Smoothing her skirt beneath her, she reclaimed her seat.

"Show him in, please."

When Larry exited her office, he did so with a smile that told Cassandra the jig was up. How much more obvious could she have been?

She glanced down at her attire. Today, she wore a plain gray suit, designed more for comfort than pizzazz. She wished she had worn one of her special-cut, form-fitting numbers. If only she had known he was coming.

"That's my job," August said, sauntering in.

She looked up into the face she had grown accustomed to seeing only at night. When the dark shadows played against the chiseled bone structure, it took her breath away. But here, in the fluorescent light of an office building she could see every perfect feature.

"What is?"

"Examining your body. I saw you checking yourself out." He took a seat across from her desk.

Cassandra smiled. "I was wishing I had worn something else. Something more eye catching."

"You could wear a burlap bag, and I'd still think you were the sexiest woman on the planet."

Suddenly she felt tingly. "When you said you were going to call, I thought you meant on the phone."

"I did, at first. And then I thought, what the hell? So, I came to see how the other half works." August's dark eyes surveyed the room. He seemed to take it all in. And then he focused on the large windows behind her desk.

"May I?" he asked.

"Be my guest."

He got up from his seat and walked behind her. He propped himself against the wall and looked out. Cassandra watched his intense stare. Finally, he broke the silence.

"It looks the same."

"What does?" she asked.

He extended his arm. She rose from her chair and joined him at the window.

"The city. It looks the same from your world, too."

Then he turned from the window to her. That tingling sensation she had earlier returned with a vengeance. Oh God, she wanted this man. She wanted him right now, this very moment, in her office. The next thing she knew, her mouth was greedily searching for his. He obliged her pursuit and parted his lips when her tongue sought entrance. She felt as though she was swimming in the oasis of his mouth. With every second she was losing herself.

"Two days early! How ya like me now!"

Jairus's voice cut through Cassandra's urgency, and she slowly withdrew from the lip lock she had on August.

The accountant smiled and lifted a curious eyebrow. "I'm sorry.

Larry wasn't at his desk, and I didn't know you had someone in your office."

"That's alright," she said, feeling her heart rate gradually returning to normal. "Jairus Flemming, this is August Knight."

August came around Cassandra's desk and met the large man halfway. They shook hands.

"Glad to meet you, August."

"Same here. Jair-us is it?"

"Yes."

"If I'm not mistaken, that's a biblical name."

Jairus nodded his agreement. "But instead of getting into that long story, I'll just leave my report and get out of your way."

He put the folder he was carrying on Cassandra's desk and headed toward the door. "Two days early," he said, without looking back.

And then he was gone.

August looked at Cassandra nearly expressionless. "You got history with him?"

She frowned but didn't lie. "Yes. But how...?"

"Men always know," he said, returning to the window. He stared in the direction of the Brookhaven construction site. "It's primal. We can smell it."

She joined him again. "Well, it is history. And besides, it's not like I've given you roses or anything."

August smiled, and they both laughed.

For the next couple of hours, the two sat and talked in Cassandra's office. She held the lion's share of the conversation, describing her early years as a merchant processing clerk and how she worked her way through school to earn a BS in business management. Then, she had set her sights on the "big chair" as her colleagues called it.

She talked about having a mentor and what a difference that made early in her career. She had no intentions of disclosing so much about herself, but by the time she felt a lull in the conversation, she had shared with August every major career path she had taken that led her finally to the coveted title of CEO.

She couldn't read his reaction. He appeared to be not so much listening as considering—weighing in the facts. And surprisingly, she was interested in his assessment. For years, Cassandra divested herself from the opinions of others. They were often uninformed or inaccurate. But the activity going on behind August's eyes intrigued her. She wanted to extend her access beyond his body and into his head.

Before she could inquire, Larry's customary two-rap knock came at her office door.

She smiled at August, then turned toward the door. "Come in."

"Is there anything else you need today, Ms. Hearst?"

"Why? Are you leaving?"

"Yes, ma'am. It's five o'clock."

"What!" Cassandra turned quickly to the wall clock behind her. The hands indeed proclaimed quitting time.

Her adrenaline surged. "Good Christ! I had a three o'clock conference call with the Omaha Center."

"I took the liberty of changing that appointment to ten A.M.. tomorrow."

She was somewhat relieved but still uneasy. "I also had a 4:30 meeting with Brigette Holmes that…"

"You now have a luncheon meeting with Ms. Holmes tomorrow at Irene's Bistro."

Cassandra covered her heart with her hand. The tom-tom in her chest settled back to a normal rhythm. "Lawrence Hayes, don't you ever leave my side."

He smiled and tipped his head. "Good evening, Ms. Hearst, Mr. Knight." He closed the door behind him.

"Where did you find him?" August asked.

"I didn't really. He found me."

"How's that?"

"We clerked together in the Merchant Services department. He must have caught wind of my ambitions. We sort of made the climb together. Larry has an associate's degree in office management. When he graduated, he asked me to remember him when I got to the top. And I did."

She could tell by the look in his eyes that he approved. She liked the feeling it gave her.

"I apologize for keeping you from your appointments. I've over-stayed my welcome."

"No," she said, reassuring him. "You haven't. I'm just usually on top of things. I should have been more conscious of my schedule." Truth be told, Cassandra was quite bothered by her irresponsibility. Nothing like that had ever happened to her. What was so compelling about this man that caused her to lose all business sense?

When August stood, she had her answer. Even in his easygoing attire, he looked regal and commanding. And that, plus their sexual exploits had captured her attention this afternoon and thrown her whole groove out of whack.

"I'd better be going."

"You're looking Land's End–casual today," she commented, ignoring his remark about leaving. She wasn't quite ready for their time together to end.

He smiled in response.

"How much time do you have?"

He licked his lips. "As much as you need."

"Good," she said. "Come on."

They walked outside of Cassandra's office. Most of the employees were gone. Those who were left were packing up.

"People sure make it a point to leave on time around here," he remarked.

"I like it that way. Unless we're under the pressure of bringing on several new banking clients at once, I encourage my people to go home on time."

"I wish I could say the same about my boss."

They weaved their way through the maze of cubicles.

"For me, it's a quality-of-worklife issue. Besides, if I treat my employees right, they in turn treat the clients right."

"And DirectData continues to rack up the big bucks."

"And DirectData continues to rack up the big bucks," she echoed.

She gave him a sideways glance. The space taken up by the cubicles narrowed the department walkways. This forced the two to walk close together. The proximity warmed Cassandra from the inside out. She felt as though she had just eaten the hottest enchilada on the planet and it was causing internal combustion. She would not have been surprised to see smoke coming out from between her legs. She stopped in front of the department.

"This is the client services center," she said, grateful that she was far away from where the last of the employees were exiting. She didn't know how well it would go over if they saw August's fingers in her hair and how much she was enjoying having them there.

"It's the heart of the business," she continued. "That's why I moved this department to the top floor with me, because...I...oh..."

August's lips brushed feather-light kisses against the back of her neck. "Because I want to stay connected to the people who actually do the work...Aug—"

Before she could finish saying his name, he pulled her into his arms and into his kiss. This man of few words communicated volumes with his body. The sweet assault of his tongue over her lips and down her neck told her that they may not make it to the motel tonight.

"Not here," she moaned, breaking free of his seduction. "Come on," she said, grabbing his hand.

They walked to the fire exit, and she took a pass card from her pocket. She waved it across a magnetic card reader and heard the hard click of the stairwell door as it unlocked. Once inside, the door whooshed closed behind them. The fact that they were alone in the stairwell brought Cassandra up to full arousal. August must have felt the same, because they grabbed each other with such fury and passion there could have easily been an electric discharge flying out from their impact.

In seconds, they were half out of their clothes and down on the carpeted landing.

"Help me," she said, unbuttoning her skirt. August flipped her over, unzipped her skirt, then quickly relieved her of it. She was about to turn over, when August stopped her.

"No," he said, sounding sensuously baritone. "I want you like this."

Cassandra raised slightly to position herself on her hands and knees. August hastily rolled on a Sentinal extra large condom and entered her from the rear.

"Umm," he moaned, knowing he'd never felt anything so exquisite in his entire life. The angle of her opening fit him precisely and felt like a welcome fist tightening around his Knight stick.

He reached around her slim waist and immersed his hand in an ocean of her wetness. It seemed that the risk of them being discovered excited them both.

With each movement in and out of her soft core, he rubbed her clit and rolled a nipple. It wasn't long before her urgent moans filled the stairwell. As her internal muscles closed down around him, he added his own moans to hers, until the stairwell filled with a Niagara of pants, groans, and gasps.

August took her faster, bumping and pulling her wildly against him. He thrust back and forth now feeling the cooling rush of release begin from the center of his balls.

Just then the sound of a door opening a floor above and subsequent footsteps startled them. But the thought of someone discovereing their tryst only stirred the caldron boiling inside him. Cassandra was similarly affected as she cried out in anticipation of the pleasure about to consume her.

At that, the footsteps stopped, but August and Cassandra were too far gone to care. First Cassandra yielded to her searing need as her body vibrated with liquid lightning. August, only seconds behind her, plunged hard and deep, while passion stronger than he had ever known hurtled him past the point of no return.

They both cried out in fulfillment and afterward heard the footsteps retreat back up the stairs. They toppled over onto the thin, silver-blue carpet, sweaty and satisfied.

"Why did you really come here today?" she asked, stroking his head.

"To see you in your element."

"Why?"

"Because there's nothing more erotic than a powerful woman."

Chapter Nine

Cassandra usually thought that one of the best aspects of her job was traveling, but not today. Anything that would take her away from August's conquests of her body would be torture. It was as if her pussy had become addicted to August's dick. And going any extended length of time without it put her through extreme withdrawal symptoms.

She looked around the plane at the few passengers boarding ahead of her. Luckily, there weren't many people traveling into Omaha tonight. So she decided to take her chances with a seat in the back. Maybe no one would disturb her there, and she could relax by stretching out on the empty seats. A restful sleep might take away some of her excess lust.

She counted twenty-four people on the small plane. So far, it looked like she would have the back all to herself. She rose and retrieved a pillow and a blanket from the overhead bin and prepared to stretch out for the ride.

When she sat down, she saw a passenger boarding. Oh no, she thought as he made his way to the back of the plane. To her chagrin, he sat in the last row with her but on the other side of the plane. "Damn," she mumbled and turned to look out of the window.

It wasn't long before the plane took off and headed south toward

Nebraska. DirectData had a small regional office there, and it was time for their yearly sales meeting. Cassandra always tried to attend any large event that the regional offices held. They usually occurred over a weekend, and then she was back to work on Monday. This trip was the same.

To prevent as much jet lag as possible, Cassandra always took the red-eye out of Minneapolis and slept on the way there. For some reason that combination made her fresh and ready for the next day's activities. Keeping this in mind, she propped her pillow against the window, covered herself with the blanket, and closed her eyes.

She was asleep almost instantaneously, but she was not resting. Visions of August ravaging her body troubled her dreams. So real were the hands that stroked her breasts. So real was the tongue marching through her pubic hair. So real was his breathing—heavy with lust and arousal.

Startled, she awoke. Her hand was between her legs and her clit was throbbing. But the breathing continued softly near her. She turned to the left to see that it was the man seated across the aisle from her who was making the sound she heard. He was breathing heavily, and she could see that although a blanket was covering him from the waist down, his hand was moving up and down on his lap. Cassandra sat transfixed as she saw the man work his shaft vigorously. His mouth was open, and he was staring at her. She pulled down the blanket with one hand to reveal were her other hand was nestled between her legs. The man licked his lips and jerked himself faster. Cassandra replaced the blanket, but not before putting her hand down into her panties and inserting her fingers into her eager opening. She matched the man's rhythm as he pulled and tugged at himself. She plunged her fingers deeper and deeper into the recesses of her core until the sounds of her wetness joined the man's moans.

The passengers closest to them looked back a couple of times, but Cassandra didn't care. She needed to relieve herself in the worst way, and she couldn't wait another moment to do it.

"Come here," the man said, pulling at himself harder and harder.

Cassandra did as she was asked and sat in the seat next to him. He spread his blanket across them both and guided her sopping fingers to his shaft. Then he inserted his fingers into her, and they resumed their stimulation. This time it was her turn to breathe hard. Within minutes she was a quivering mass of satedness as the stranger's hand made her explode like fireworks in July. Then as the captain's voice filled the cabin announcing the approach of 30,000 feet, the man's penis erupted, and a thick, warm liquid oozed down the sides of Cassandra's hand. This could possibly be the most exciting business trip she had ever taken.

One thing she liked about Omaha was the size of things. Her $70 per night room would have cost at least $500 per night in New York—$200 per night in Minneapolis. The room-service meal she had earlier cost $18 and provided enough food for two people to get full. And finally the size of the enthusiasm of the people in the city was one for the record books. People she didn't even know offered her warm greetings and talked with her sometimes as if they'd known her for years. And the dairy farms and ranches of outlying areas away from the cities ensured that each meal came fresh and delicious.

Cassandra turned off the television in her hotel room and sighed.

The sales conference was over early, but not early enough for her to go sightseeing. She would have liked to visit Malcolm X's birth site again, but instead she went down to the hotel gift shop in search of a magazine. After looking around a bit, she saw a new novel by one of her favorite authors, Kim Louise. She paid for the book and headed back to her room where she would pass the next hour or so reading until it was time for her to head to the airport.

Cassandra was a nonlinear reader. She often skipped around to some of the juicy parts of a book before settling in for the entire story.

Today was no exception as her eyes skimmed the pages of the historical novel *Queen of Hearts* for something lustful.

Before long, she was reading from page 110 where the hero and heroine were getting their first taste of each other.

Tate scooped Corene into his arms and carried her brazenly up the stairs. With his longing for her now at its peak, he barely registered her fists pounding against his chest.

"Unhand me, you brute!"

He reached the top of the stairs and headed toward his bedchamber. "I've finished toying with you. And now, by all the gods, I will have you!"

Corene recoiled in shock. "You wouldn't dare."

He dropped her onto the firm bedding and ripped open his shirt. "Don't protest now, your majesty."

As Corene stared in amazement, Tate removed one article of clothing after another until, at last, he stood before her naked and bulging. Her eyes widened. Never before had she seen such a magnificent specimen. More perfect than Michealangelo's David, yet chiseled nonetheless. All the flirtations in the empire could not have prepared her for this golden-brown mammoth of a man.

"I see we understand each other," he said, joining her on the massive pallet.

"Lieutenant Bearden, you can't possibly be serious."

He placed his full weight on top of her. When she gasped, he smiled. "All of my mistresses call me Tate. As for my seriousness…" He ground his rigid erection against her quivering thighs.

"I order you to…"

Tate's lips caught hers midsentence. He parted her mouth and sent his tongue probing for the delicacies of the soft flesh inside. All of the wanton looks she had given him, all of the coincidental brushes against his skin, and all of the unusual ways in which they found themselves alone had to mean something. He was determined to find out what.

Her body softened and yielded to his. She returned his kiss, and the fire he'd sometimes seen blazing in her eyes now passed between them like an inferno. So, she was not just a flirtatious vixen after all, he mused. Perhaps she was indeed capable of feeling something other than power and greed.

With her eager assistance, he disrobed her, then marveled at the curves and valleys of her body.

"Hurul-ayni," he whispered. And without another word, he entered her. He knew it was too soon, but he also knew that if he had waited another second, he would have been in danger of spilling himself on her royal stomach.

Once inside, he remained still to cool his impetuousness. However the elliptical hip movements of Sovereign Corene Jalay told him that she was now the impatient one.

Tate sucked in a sharp breath and wondered where his bravado had gone. Just a moment ago, he had the aggression of ten men. And now the slightest movement from her majesty had reduced him to a gasping fool.

He remained still while her hips circled and rocked him. And to think he believed he had taken her too soon. By the measure of her extreme wetness, it was he who had been taken.

"Corene," he said, closing his eyes.

She arched her back slightly and continued the hypnotic drumming of her thighs. Her muscles tightened and released around him, and he lost himself to their sweet torture.

Still immobile, he collapsed against her firm breasts. "Ah, ah."

"Why, lieutenant Bearden, it's so unlike you to be this malleable."
Her fingers danced a sensuous staccato across his back, where the muscles there were as hard as granite.

She whispered into his ear. "Wasn't this your idea?"

She was pulling on him, stroking him like a firm hand. No woman had ever manipulated him so deftly. And he'd had professionals—women whose reputations were grand and pricey. But this siren, ruler of Elandra, had talents above them all. And he, first lieutenant of the queen's army, was vanquished.

That's enough soldier, *he thought.* You cannot allow yourself to succumb to this, this…female rampage. *Slowly, he opened his eyes and summoned his remaining self-mastery.* You are Tatenham Heart, III, captain of the guard. And she, *he stared down into eyes the color of nightshade,* is the enemy.

Corene lifted her buttocks and shifted her hips slightly. At the same time, Tate grabbed one of her legs and wrapped it around his waist.

"Oh!" she gasped.

He grinned. "Did you think I was going to let you have all the fun?"

Tate took her other leg and wrapped it around him as well, and then he started, ever so slowly, to pump himself in and out of her soaked center.

"Lieutenant, I..."

"Ah, ah, ah," he responded. "It's my turn to talk."

The old wooden floorboards creaked with Tate's movements. Corene's eyes widened.

"But first..." Tate lowered his mouth to hers and kissed her zealously. He imagined that her lips were a pomegranate, her tongue was the delicate meat inside, and that he was a starving man. The vision made him delirious with hunger.

He pillaged her mouth like a vandal. All the while, moving gradually in and out of her. And then he heard it. It started thinly, like a vapor. Then steadily it increased in intensity until it became a whimper beneath him and then a moan. Finally he heard Corene cry out. And he knew he had become master over the domain of her body.

"Lieutenant," she murmured.

"Tate," he corrected, and continued his resolute possession of her. "Why have you tormented me so?" he asked.

There was no answer. Only heavy breathing.

"Like a great plaque, you have infected my mind."

He stroked her face and drove deeper into the center of her thighs. "Why did you tease me into madness?"

Corene's only response came in the form of deep sobs. He slipped his hands beneath her round rear and lifted her toward him.

"Why, my queen?"

He thrust himself into her farther and faster. With tears streaming down her face, she matched the depth and fury of his rhythm.

"Why!" he demanded, bracing himself for the impending explosion from his loins into hers.

"Because I love you!" she shot back and shattered like glass into a million shimmering pieces.

Cassandra closed the book with a smile on her face. She was going to enjoy reading the rest of it. Kim's books always made her horny. This one was no exception. Too bad there wasn't enough time for her to relieve herself of the buildup caused by the sensual story. *Oh well,* she thought. *It'll have to wait until I get back home to August. He'll free my pent-up yearning,* she thought.

Chapter Ten

Nervous would not be an accurate description of what Cassandra felt. The closest she could come to naming what she was experiencing was performance anxiety. *If this is what men go through,* she thought, applying powder to her face, *then it's a miracle they can get it up at all.*

There was a time when she would have looked in the mirror and whispered, "Flawless." But as she examined the reflection she saw, the only word that she could think to whisper was *hoochie*. "Look at me," she said. "In my *Waiting to Exhale* dress and my Frederick's of Hollywood pumps." She thought she looked like a woman on a man-hunt.

She left her expansive bathroom and went on one more walk-through of her home. She adored her bi-level overlook. It resembled a small ski lodge with its dark wood and large, round cobblestones making up the outside frame and its cozy yet spacious inside. The ceilings were high, the fireplaces were numerous, and the view was spectacular. It had far more rooms than she would ever need. But she had fallen in love at first sight.

Because of her hectic lifestyle and her utter distaste for house-work, she had hired a maid service when she first moved in. But, when she and August set a dinner date at her place, she had spent three evenings cleaning her home from loft to rec room. She was pleased with her final inspection and headed to the kitchen to check the meal.

Figuring August to be a meat-and-potatoes man, she had prepared Yankee pot roast with new potatoes and candied carrots. She would start them off with spaghetti salad and the finishing touch would be pecan pie. With August bringing the wine, she anticipated a savory meal.

Reviewing a mental checklist, Cassandra went over the last of her preparations. The table was set with dinnerware from Tiffany & Co., a small silk flower arrangement, and two long-stemmed candles. Fresh ylang-ylang and musk potpourri permeated each room. The ceiling fans were on and turning the fragrant air. More candles lined the headboard of her king-size waterbed, which was complete with fresh linen in a brushstroke pattern. And her favorite CD, one she had burned herself, which included all of Luther's love songs, was in the stereo waiting to be played.

She checked the time: 6:52. Eight minutes, she thought. For the last two days, her body had ached with need. She'd put in so much overtime on the new software conversion project, that she and August hadn't been able to reconcile their schedules. And now, Cassandra was again suffering from withdrawal symptoms of not having August's body all over hers.

The doorbell rang, and her heart shifted into third gear. She willed herself to calm down, but she couldn't wait to see him. Her memory of what his mere touch could do sent a warm shiver to her lower body. *What that man does brings the woman all the way out of me,* she mused, sauntering toward her large wooden front door. She struck a seductive pose and swung the door open.

"Damn."

"Does that mean you like what you see?"

The two days he had been waiting to see this woman had driven him crazy. An eternity had passed since he had tasted her. He felt fully alive and powerful. His heartbeat thundered in his ears.

"Well?" she asked.

He grabbed her quickly and forcefully. Then he devoured her mouth and felt his passion grow strong as her body went weak against his. She tasted supernatural. She smelled like every flower on earth, and she felt like a monsoon. The more his tongue teased and probed, the more she moaned and drew herself closer until there was no air between them.

When she pulled away, he groaned loudly.

"Come inside," she said, in a voice one measure above a whisper.

He stepped inside, and she closed the door behind him.

This time it was Cassandra's turn to be the aggressor. Before August could blink, her lips had captured his and her hands traveled the length of his back and down where they rested on his buttocks. He could tell he'd been missed.

He closed his arms around her and settled in. Several moments passed before either of them pulled away. August was the first to step back. He wanted to get a good look at the almost-dress she was wearing before he removed it.

"Welcome to my home," she said, catching her breath. "Let me show you the place."

"Are you kidding?"

She tried to walk away, and he pulled her back to where he stood.

"Woman, I've been waiting two days for you." August looked down to where the proof of his anguish was rising.

"If you've waited two days, you can wait two more hours."

"Two hours!"

She took his hand and led him into the living room. "Yes, two hours. Come on."

After she put away the wine he'd brought, he followed her from room to room. Cassandra's living space was impressive. From the cathedral ceilings to the large bay windows and sunken living room, the house was built for expansive, luxurious lifestyle. The structural design was familiar to him.

"This is a Madigrill," he offered.

"A what?" she asked, walking him down a long hallway.

"Jim Madigrill is the architect. I recognize his work."

She smiled.

"Just down here to the left should be the master bedroom."

"You're right. So what do you think?"

They entered the large room and stood close together. The heat from their bodies intensified at the sight of the inviting boudoir.

"I think I can't wait," he said, rubbing her shoulders.

She rested her hands upon his. "Then let's eat."

"Cassandra," he said, pulling her into his arms once again. "Your home is spectacular, and I'm grateful for the tour." His hands roamed her body freely, circling her breasts and occasionally brushing past a nipple. "But what I'm hungry for I can't get out of that kitchen."

He planted a stream of gentle kisses, starting from her temple and then on down the side of her neck and to her cleavage.

Cassandra moaned. "If you don't stop, I'm going to have to go put on some underwear."

"That does it!" he declared, imagining her hips naked beneath her clothing. And that beautiful dark triangle...

Lust took over his actions, and he lifted her into his arms and marched off toward the bed.

"August," she protested.

"Don't ask me to stop, Dark Lady. Please."

Her dress was tied loosely in the front. It was secured just enough to expose various areas of smoky brown flesh, round and calling to him. He made quick work of undoing the bow.

"If we start this now, dinner will be ruined."

The seriousness in her eyes told him that she must have gone through a lot of trouble to prepare dinner. He kissed her forehead and relented.

His aggressive behavior embarrassed him. "I'm sorry if I came on too strongly." He pulled Cassandra up from the bed.

"Don't apologize. Believe me, I know."

He saw the evidence of her arousal as her nipples jutted out against the bodice of her dress. He watched her hands retying the front strings.

"No, don't. With it open, it looks like a promise."

"I like that." She smiled.

August gestured toward the dining area. "Shall we go?"

She walked in front of him, and he memorized the movement of her thighs. Two hours, he thought, sighing.

Cassandra asked him to take a seat at the table as she prepared their plates.

In minutes, the aromas from the kitchen started a chain reaction within him. By the time she emerged with the salads, he was famished. They ate in silence and finished quickly.

"Ready for more," she asked.

"I'm always ready for more," he responded.

She took their salad bowls into the kitchen. After a few moments, she returned with two plates heaping with meat and vegetables. They dug in heartily.

"You really seem to love what you do," she said.

August remembered the last time he heard her scream and smiled flirtatiously. "You got that right."

"I mean your job, silly."

"Oh," he said, laughing. "That, too."

August ate his food enthusiastically. His brain registered that it was good—delicious in fact. But his concentration held on Cassandra. The way she ate her food fascinated him. From the delicate yet deliberate way she lifted her fork to the way her lips parted expectantly to receive it. From the way her mouth closed around the tender morsels of meat to the gentle way she slid the fork away from her mouth. August imagined pieces of himself savored by her oral juices.

She even chewed her food with a rhythm not unlike their love-making. There was no way on this Earth he would wait two hours to have her. He couldn't.

"August?"

"Yes," he said, smiling knowingly.

"Where were you?"

"Inside you," he admitted honestly. "Where I should be."

He saw her face warm with his words and knew she agreed.

"I was asking about your job. What's it like moving those big cranes around?"

"Powerful," he responded, watching her spear a carrot. "Sometimes I feel like I can move the world."

"Have you always worked in a construction yard?"

Carefully, she pinched a piece from her roll. August's eyes watched her hands. It was like seeing angels dance. "Since I was a kid."

"Your dedication impresses me," she said, raising the glass of wine to her lips. She took a small sip. "Your parents must be very proud."

"My old man has his chest puffed out, but my mother's a different story. She keeps wondering when I'm going to get a real job." August smiled, taking a sip from his own wineglass.

"Is that hard for you?"

"Naw. She doesn't give me a hard time. Early in my career, my pops wanted me to join him in the yard, and my mother wanted me to go to college. So I compromised. I got a degree in engineering, and as soon as a graduated, I went to work with my father."

"Do you still work with him?"

"No. He retired four years ago. So, now my folks spend a lot of their time traveling. I hardly see them anymore."

August frowned and shook his head.

"What?" Cassandra asked.

"I'm usually a man of few words. I can't believe I'm telling you all this."

Her left eyebrow rose provocatively. "Maybe it's the company."

"No doubt," he replied, finishing the last of the food on his plate. "Can I tempt you with dessert?"

He couldn't talk. He knew if he opened his mouth it would only be to explore hers. And this time there would be no stopping him. He would take her recklessly and without restraint.

When Cassandra got up from the table, he was sure she could read his mind. She took their dinner plates into the kitchen and in moments returned with a slice of pecan pie a la mode. She set the dish before him and took her seat.

"Aren't you having any?"

"I can't eat another bite."

"Really?" he said, rising.

The gaze of Cassandra's eyes traveled the length of his body and then stopped at the dessert plate he carried. He knelt beside her. "Eat with me," he said, taking a bit of pie and soft vanilla ice cream on a fork. Slowly she opened her mouth, and he fed her the sweet treat.

After taking a bite himself, he gathered more of the pie and ice cream on the fork. He watched intently as the utensil slid easily in and out of her mouth. A piece of pecan hung precariously out of the side of her mouth, and August touched it lightly with his finger moving it gently toward her mouth. With her moist, sweetened lips she captured the nut and the tip of his finger. The delirious sensation immediately stiffened him as she sucked leisurely on his finger. Her mouth was hot and wet. Her tongue and teeth played with his nerve endings, and memories of their encounter in the cab of his crane made him moan.

"I do so like pleasing you, August."

She got up from her seat. "Wait here," she said.

Nearly fully aroused, August sat on the floor of her dining room and finished off the remaining dessert. Soon after, Cassandra returned with a large sheet. She pushed aside the coffee table in the living room and laid the sheet on the floor. Then she walked into the kitchen. August heard the opening and closing of a cupboard, and then she returned.

"In here," she said, helping him up.

His blood coursed with anticipation. It seemed that he wasn't going to have to wait two hours after all.

"I need you naked."

Before she finished the sentence, he was already unbuttoning his shirt. "I thought you would never ask."

He kept his eyes on hers as he removed each article of clothing. He noted the enlargement of her pupils as he removed his silk boxers. When he was fully nude, she came toward him. In his aroused state, he hadn't noticed the box of cornstarch in her hand.

"What are you going to do with that?"

"Lay down and I'll show you," she purred.

"No, really. What are you going to do with that?"

"Make you feel like heaven."

"Then come on with it," he replied, stretching out on the sheet.

His firm, sinewy muscles glowed brown-sugar brown in the candlelight. Cassandra smiled inside. His invitation was strong.

"First, your back," she said, hoping to free her eyes from the intoxicating sight of his male member in full salute.

"Whatever you say," he said, and turned over onto his stomach.

She knelt beside him. "I say relax, August Knight."

As she sprinkled the cornstarch onto her hands, she heard him release a long, slow breath.

Cassandra set the box aside and rubbed her hands together. Then she pressed her hands against his shoulders and slid her palms across their wide berth.

His skin was the softest thing she had ever touched. She moaned, pressing outward to the sides of his torso, making circles toward his heart.

"Umm, harder, baby," he responded.

She leaned in closer, adding more of her weight. She spread more of the cornstarch down to his lower back.

"Yes," he responded.

Cassandra applied more cornstarch to her hands and continued her exploration of August's body.

Having spent sufficient time on his back, she moved lower to pay tribute to his tightly packed and symmetrically round butt. She moved her hands over the mounds, down the sides, and then back toward the crack. August spread his legs so she could get her fingers between the delicious split. Slowly she worked from top to bottom until she heard him moan.

From there she moved on to his thighs, which were as large as tree trunks. Maintaining her deep pressure, her fingers roamed the massive upper areas then went gliding down to his calves and ankles.

She could see the faint trails of her hand prints against his body where most of the cornstarch had been rubbed in. "And now the other side," she said, voice lust-deep. The sensation of the exquisite softness made her clit throb in anticipation.

Her plan was to rub down his chest, stomach, and the front of his legs. And then finish with her damp descent onto his dark crevice. But she was too aroused. And she wondered quite strongly what his penis would feel like in her cornstarched hands. She held the box over the place where August's probing manhood lay pulsating against his lower abdomen.

"I dare you!" he said.

And with that, she sprinkled the white powder on his private part as if he were an infant. Then she began the scintillating task of rubbing it in.

She caressed him. First with one hand and then another. A warm current of adrenaline traveled from her fingertips to her valley. The feeling was rapturous.

"Szzz, ah," August moaned and began to move his hips in time with her long strokes. Even though her hands slid effortlessly up and down his lust-stiffened shaft, she gripped him tighter and tighter. August reached for her breasts and massaged them strongly while Cassandra worked him faster and faster.

"Damn, baby," August cried out, jerking upward. "Damn."

She continued sliding quickly, and then with her free hand, she cupped his balls and manipulated them.

"Oh, shit!" he responded as a stream of semen shot up and covered the back of Cassandra's hand.

He drew his breath in deep and heavy gulps. "You must...come to my house...so I can return...the favor."

Chapter Eleven

The now seasoned couple walked arm-in-arm down the hallway of August's apartment building. They were laughing like teenagers at some silly joke Cassandra made as August fumbled with his key.

The door across the hall opened, and a woman stared, fuming, at the giggling twosome.

"Well, well, well. And I suppose you're going to tell me that I've got it all wrong and this isn't what it seems."

August looked solemnly at Maxine. "No. This is exactly what it seems."

The woman rolled her eyes and slammed her door closed.

"Ex-girlfriend?"

"Not even."

"Good."

They entered August's apartment, and Cassandra's heart quickened like the footwork in *Riverdance*. "I want you."

August's chestnut-brown eyes darkened to a smoldering ebon. "Show me," he replied.

She came after him with wanton disregard for restraint. He relinquished himself to her wild embrace.

No more substitutes, Cassandra thought tearing his shirt free of sinewy arm muscles. *No more Tongue Teasers, no more stories about rings.* Cassandra let August come up for air briefly, and then devoured him again. *No more finger jobs from strangers or romance novels. This,* she thought digging her nails into his back, *is the real deal. No one or nothing has ever made me feel the way August does.* She reveled in the strong embrace of his arms as he lifted her and carried her into his bedroom.

At first, he wanted to be around her, because he wanted to have sex. Now he found himself wanting to be around her simply because he wanted to be around her. He wasn't sure when it happened. Only that it had. Looking at her now told him that their typical wham bam was out of the question. He wanted to take his time with her. Savor her. Immerse himself in her.

"What?" she asked, looking up.

He stroked her hair. "I'm gonna do you slow," he said.

Cassandra's heart fluttered. "W-what?"

He kissed her forehead, left cheek, then the right. "I think we just might pull an all-nighter."

"August," she protested. "I just want to…"

"Not tonight," he responded and kissed her with all the tenderness in his heart. It was a long, lingering, deep, soul-opening kiss. Cassandra was overwhelmed. August wanted more.

She tried to resist. She knew if he did what he said, it would topple her like a stack of dominoes. Her feelings would forever be spread out, face up, for all to see.

She wriggled against him, but he persisted.

"Let me," he said, grinding his hips softly against hers.

And then the first domino came crashing down from the stack. "Let me love you," he said, claiming her lips.

Suddenly, she was Sheba, on a throne of gold, both sovereign and subject of devoted worship. He had placed her body upon an alter of down—his lips and hands a burnt offering against her skin.

She wanted more and was selfish in her taking, opening her arms, her legs, and her soul to his unabashed wanderings.

Each tender taste of her flesh hefted her senses skyward. She breathed deeply, her nostrils expanded with the fragrance of his skin.

His hands were everywhere stroking, kneading, ravishing. Within moments, Cassandra came undone.

As the tips of his fingers brushed feather-light back and forth across her ripe nipples, August questioned the force that compelled him. All day he felt caged like a panther in captivity. Waiting for his freedom to come in the form of a woman's body. His woman's body. The realization hit him like a slap. His urgent need for her. The way her body felt to him now. The stormy passion he saw in her eyes. All signs that they were doing much more than just having sex.

"August," she whispered.

His name came out hot and breathy against his cheek. The sensation sent him driving farther into the soft, warm center of her womanspace. He pushed deeper to get more and more of himself inside her. She arched her back to accommodate him.

He straightened himself above her and lifted her legs until her heels rested on his shoulders. Like the moon's effect on the tides of the ocean, her influence on him was inescapable. He leaned forward, inching himself toward her.

Her hips ground themselves aggressively against his. He wanted to tell her exactly what he was feeling but he was too emotion-filled to speak.

His raw sensuousness carried her to greater heights. She could feel the heat of his body course down the entire length of hers. He increased the pace of their joining only slightly and waves of ecstasy throbbed through her.

They were one, one being, one heart. One pulse. He was not just her lover anymore. August was part of her now, and that thought intensified her passion beyond all reason.

Now the dominoes fell in pairs, in threes. She was losing the battle. He said it. But she felt it. She was falling in love. He was taking her over, and she wasn't sure if she would ever be able to find her way back.

Large tears slid down the sides of her face. "August, please," she pleaded.

He looked down, eyes full of tenderness. "Do you really want me to stop."

If she lied, she could get out of it, before all the dominoes fell and she was lost to him forever. She wanted to lie. She opened her mouth to lie. But the ocean moving inside her wouldn't let her.

"No."

August closed his eyes and dropped his head. And then he changed the rhythm of his movement from soft thrusts to a circular motion. It was so slow, it was barely perceptible. By the time his hips made their first rotation, Cassandra was sobbing and cumming. Her muscles contracted around his hard manhood. August moaned deeply.

He took her long into the night. Just when she thought that an orgasm was about to put an end to his pleasuring, he would slow himself to a snail's pace that seemed to reset him, yet took her swiftly into ecstasy. She had given up fighting it. And all her dominoes were long gone.

She wrapped her arms tighter around his neck and stared up into his eyes. She saw a fire blazing there. One she hoped matched the inferno growing in her heart. He kept his promise. All night he had been inside her, moving, mating, taking away her restraint.

He gasped in sweet agony. "A-ah, Cassandra." His slow pace was replaced by a quicker tempo. More moans filled the air. Strong, firm thrusts conquered the space between her thighs. She held on tightly, determined to go with him wherever he led. She was his. She knew that now. When she felt August pulsing inside her, the sensation took her over for yet another trembling release.

Oh, God, she thought, realizing her predicament. *What do I do* now?

"I love you," he said and kissed her forehead.

"You what!"

He looked into her eyes as if he was trying to find himself in them. "I said I love you."

The last person who had said those words to her was Jairus. Then, she had been too wrapped up in her career to make room for love. And now what? she wondered. There's still so much she wanted to do.

"I don't think now is a good time," she began.

August rolled off her and laid beside her on his bed.

"I've got news for you. Falling in love is not something you can just schedule in your appointment book. It happens when it happens, and it can't be asked to hold on line three or told to wait outside your office or filed away in your desk. You simply wake up one day, and there it is. Even though it's been building itself over time.

"Have you ever driven past something, a fast-food restaurant or a parking garage, and thought, *When did that get there?* 'cause it seems like it popped up overnight. Well the truth is, Cassandra, we've both been there constructing this thing between us, only maybe we didn't know it. So now that it's here, we can't ignore it. Baby, we can't."

"For a man of few words, I can't believe you said all that."

"They say love does strange things."

"I guess they're right."

August wrapped his arm around her shoulders. "Just sleep on it," he said. "Let me know how you feel in the morning."

It was the fifth time that morning that Cassandra had rearranged the items on her desk. Instead of preparing for her project update meeting, she relocated her penholder, desk pad, retrieval box, and in basket to various places, never satisfied.

Aggravated, she got up from her New York Library–style chair and paced her expansive six-hundred-square-foot office. Her foot-falls dull and muffled into thickly padded carpet, she walked back and forth past walls proudly displaying plaque after plaque of her accomplishments. Although she kept her degrees at home, the educational certificates and designations she'd earned were impressive in her office. There were several from the banking and finance industry. Several others from the management field. Then there were individual awards she'd received from the NAACP, the Twin Cities Chamber of Commerce, and the National Black Women in Business Association.

She stopped mid-stride realizing that despite all her accolades and achievements, she had become a woman wrung out by a man. August had single handedly stripped her naked of all her business acumen and left her like a love sick teenager. Well, actually, she thought, he had accomplished that feat using both hands and his tongue, among other things.

"Look at Miss Peacock. You are truly strutting your stuff around here. What's the deal?"

Cassandra faked ignorance. "Why, Jairus, whatever do you mean?" The large man came into Cassandra's office bearing an expansive grin.

"Do you have any idea what kinda vibe you're radiating? I over-heard Rod and Jack talking about you this morning."

Her smile broadened. She was always ready for a good compliment. "What did they say?"

"Rod said something about you looking good lately."

"And...?"

"And Jack said, 'Yeah, damn good.'"

Instead of eavesdropping on your coworkers, you just concentrate on the second-quarter financials that are due at the end of this week.

The look on Jairus's face was incredulous.

"Well," she responded, "you wouldn't want to be late."

"Have I ever?"

No. In all the years she'd known him, he had never been late.

Errant thoughts of why they hadn't been able to maintain their relationship coursed through her mind. She remembered so vividly how he had been upfront about wanting a wife and a family.

And she had made it clear that she was on the fast track. At that time, her career was her second lover. Besides, settling down sounded like something that would take the pizzazz out of what they had. So she rejected it. Eventually, Jairus moved on.

Well, she wasn't about to make the same mistake again.

"Jairus, will you excuse me? I have an important call to make."

"Sure," he said. "And Cassandra?"

"Yes," she responded, phone in hand.

"You're making the right decision."

And with that, he was gone. Cassandra dialed the numbers for August's cell phone. She let it ring several times before hanging up.

I hope it's not too late.

Just then, there was a knock at her office door. August stepped in with his hands behind his back. She smiled brightly.

"August," she said, relieved.

He walked up to her. "I know I said that I would give you some time but..."

He brought his right hand around from behind his back, and in it was a vase holding three dozen yellow roses.

"August!" she exclaimed and planted kiss after kiss on his cheek.

She had been quite impulsive lately. Perhaps it was the heat or maybe the way August called her Dark Lady. But one thing was now undeniable. She took the flowers and inhaled their fragrance deeply.

"I love you, too."

Indigo After Dark, Vol. I

By
Nia Dixon and Angelique

Like a musical director who guides an orchestra to a climactic crescendo, Nia Dixon takes you there musically, poetically, and sexually, with her collection of stories, **Midnight Erotic Fantasies.** Her poignant emphasis on female pleasure is told with such awesome detail you'll feel your temperature rising from the first story to the last. She develops a true mixture of erotic fantasies, which will send you running to find pleasure in the arms of the one you love.

In Between the Night by Angelique tells of the erotic adventures of Margaret and her sexual awakening from plain Jane by day to the sensual cat on the prowl, Jade, by night. Margaret is both frightened and intrigued by the dark and dangerous feelings that consume her. It is Anthony, a stranger she meets in the park, who brings out the real woman hidden beneath—and now he, too, is consumed by her fire.

ISBN 1-58571-050-4 $10.95
Order your *Indigo After Dark, Vol. I* today at your favorite bookstore or online at the Genesis Press Web site, www.genesis-press.com.

Indigo After Dark, Vol. II

By
Dolores Bundy & Cole Riley

Brown Sugar Diaries by **Dolores Bundy** brings you a potpourri of explicit, vividly portrayed erotic short stories that takes an exotic plunge into the vibrant lifestyles of people who go beyond a devotion to unbridled pleasure. Jump into the rhythmic Brazilian nightclub scene with Zoe, a blue-eyed, bronzed temptress whose insatiable lust for sex is sizzling and telling. Her signature song "To Zoe with Love," gives her something she can feel. Travel to Africa with Mandingo Man with Big Feet and discover the mystery behind I got my Mojo working. Fasten your seat belts. These steamy and tantalizing erotic stories are unchained, unleashed and unlimited. And there's more to cum!

The Forbidden Art of Desire by **Cole Riley** offers a dozen erotic sexcapades featuring people from a variety of backgrounds and circumstances, either in lust or love. In this collection you'll meet a trophy wife who discovers that a threesome with a stranger in Rio has unforeseen benefits for her marriage, a Wall Street career woman who gets more than she bargins for when she orders a special delivery of love, a female cabbie with a penchant for sexual hijinks who finds love in the most unusual situation, a young woman's erotic coming of age at a Parisian bookstore, and many more. In all of these tempting tales, desire is the key ingredient and spark for a sizzling sensual interlude.

ISBN 1-58571-051-2 $10.95
Order your *Indigo After Dark, Vol. II* today at your favorite bookstore or online at the Genesis Press Web site. www.genesispress.com.

Genesis-Press.com

The ultimate place for
sensuous
African American love stories
written by award winning authors.

If you haven't logged on yet then you
don't know what you're missing.
Sexy attractive couples, and excerpts
of upcoming titles.
Subscribe to receive Genesis Press'
monthly newsletter.

Come see what awaits you at
www.genesis-press.com
Indigo
Indigo After Dark
What do you want to read today?

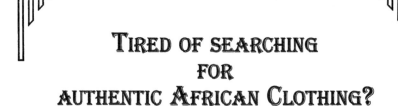

TIRED OF SEARCHING
FOR
AUTHENTIC AFRICAN CLOTHING?

Then search no more!

Saintswear International has the finest in African cloting.

We also sell 100% pure African Shea Butter.

Order online at

eSaintswear.com

Or call us at (662) 244-7144
to place your order.

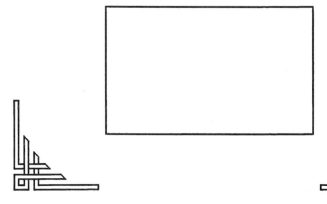

ORDER FORM

Mail to: Genesis Press, Inc.
315 3rd Avenue North
Columbus, MS 39701

Name _____

Address _____

City/State _____ Zip _____

Telephone _____

Ship to (if different from above)

Name _____

Address _____

City/State _____ Zip _____

Telephone _____

Qty.	Author	Title	Price	Total

Use this order form, or call 1-888-INDIGO-1	Total for books $ _____

	Shipping and handling:
	  $4 first two book, $1 each
	  additional books $ _____

	Total S & H $ _____
	Total amount enclosed $ _____
	Mississippi residents add 7% sales tax